THREE MEN

THREE MEN

novellas by

Nathan Leslie

*t*P
Texture Press
2017

Published in the United States by
Texture Press
1108 Westbrooke Terrace
Norman, OK 73072

For ordering information,
visit the Texture Press website at
www.texturepress.org

ISBN-13: 978-1-945784-06-4
ISBN-10: 1-945784-06-7

TABLE OF CONTENTS

Arrow East

1.

The wind swirls catching cigarette butts, candy wrappers, and crumpled fliers, tattered rags of newspaper, straws and mangled plastic bottles. Sean stands at the corner of Thirteenth and Arch Street, looking out into the line of cypress trees. The sun smears the horizon. Towhees chatter in the grimy scrub.

Sean can feel something happening, as if the Earth is preparing itself for the desertion of light. Everything follows a kind of haphazard logic, he thinks—eventually.

Sean is hoping he can catch a ride before it gets dark. He knows once darkness descends, his chances diminish precipitously. It might take him two hours after nightfall. It might take him six hours. He might not be able to snag a ride at all. That's just the way it is. Then again hitching is like anything else, Sean knows—you have to be dogged and nettlesome and a pain in the ass. Only then will luck stumble along in some exhausted form.

The wind gusts road grit against his threadbare jeans. At least the wind keeps the stench of gasoline and exhaust partially at bay. His own stink—he can live with that.

Cars stream by. Sean glances back at the Shell station, hoping one of the drivers there will see him, come to fathom his situation. He'd rather not stick his thumb out. Not that cliché. In the 21st Century he wants to act as if something new is afoot, even if it isn't. He'd like to find a different way.

Sean's orange frame backpack contains two pairs of underwear, two pairs of pants, three pairs of socks, a sweatshirt, a jacket, a wool army blanket, a knife, a fork, a spoon, a bowl, a mug, a sleeping bag, a dream journal, a toothbrush, a baseball cap, a small paperback of Renaissance paintings he found in the Dumpster, a sewing kit, a chess set and rolled-up board, cans of corn and beans, a bag of hard rolls, a bag of peanuts, a jar of sunflower seeds, apples, raisins, a small can of coffee, a Sterno stove and fuel, a small bundle of pots and pans, and a pillow the size of a small loaf of bread. Sean keeps his wallet in his left front pants pocket, and a bottle of water in the right. Inside the wallet is one hundred and fifty dollars. Around his neck Sean wears a small, cracked wooden figure of a heron, its wings spread. He thumbs it from time to time, a habit. He likes the feel of each groove, the feathers, the beak and the wings.

Also in his front pocket Sean keeps a pebble he found on the beach up near Eureka. He rotates it between his thumb and middle finger. Once he stayed up there for two weeks. Nothing on Earth like those Redwoods, Sean thinks. Those trees bear inherent significance, he thinks. We will never understand it or replicate it.

Sean can feel the straps taunt his shoulder blades. It is not an excruciating dig, though it becomes so by accretion. He can take it for some time more. For now Sean is still fresh. He's only thirty miles from Berkeley and knows he could still call a friend, easily catch a ride back. They know the score. That is a consolation. However, putting the backpack on the ground, Sean has found, is problematic and yields poor luck.

He holds his hand up, and his thumb. He holds his hand in front of his eyes, to shield them from the glare of headlights. The trucks are blinding—those piercing halogens.

Sean knows if he fails to snag a ride soon he'll have to slog into the field behind the gas station and take his chances nesting in the high grasses. But it rained last night. He would rather not sleep in a grubby hole. Sean has done this over and over, but his hitching game feels tarnished. He knows you have to be insistent, you have to want it, and Sean lacks the will to summon the energy—the one thing he has in short supply.

Sean is wearing his favorite pair of jeans, which over the past year or so has become covered with brown and grey stains and they taper off into rags. He wears a black hooded sweatshirt. His canvas tennis shoes are ripped and raveled. He hasn't eaten since nine in the morning—a banana and some recently expired yogurt. He hasn't showered in three days and he can smell and feel the need. His skin itches and burns slightly.

Sean is only twenty-one, but he feels older. He has always felt older—though he wonders if that is a projection, some kind of bastard trickery of the mind. Some dreamscape.

An hour and a half later Sean hears a car bleat at him. The car idles behind him at the station. This after the backpack rests next to him. So much for superstition.

"Hey, what's-your-name? I remember *you*." The man is tall, gangly, and very blonde. Probably in his forties, or so. He's wearing an electric blue track suit with orange stripes. His face is gaunt and Sean can see the assembly of his skull. From a distance, the man's hair appears white in the gas station lights. The man shoves the pump back into its holster and leans against his green jeep. His eyes look unoccupied, as if he's not fully *there*. His skin is pale, almost translucent and his face seems placid, almost stunned. Sean remembers the pictures of cave-dwelling lizards he saw in school. Splayed fingers and large eyes.

Sean tells him, and the man says, "I *know* you. I remember you." Sean nods. He heard him the first time.

"You live in Antioch, right?"

"No, it's Berkeley. Closer to El Cerrito, really. We met?"

The man pulls something out of his pocket. He waves Sean over to the jeep. The man holds out his hand. Sean wonders if the man has a pigment issue, something with his skin. Sean isn't sure, however, and doesn't want to ask. He has learned not to ask too many questions.

The man holds a viewfinder, the kind Sean remembers from the beach. The lifeguards would sell them towel to towel. This one is blue, with a yellow ring around the opening. It has a silver chain around the other side, but the viewfinder isn't linked to anything. Sean smells an odd bestial odor emanating from the man's jeep. A musky smell, but sour and pungent.

"I think you'll appreciate this," the man says. He turns his hand into Sean's. "Look." Sean lifts the viewfinder to his eye and holds it up to the gas station light. He closes his other eye. Inside the viewfinder a golden speckled cat leaps in the air, claws outstretched, ready for the kill. The background is an almost blinding white. Sean can see the shiny teeth of the cat, the eyes and the whiskers. Sean thinks of Joey, his old family cat. He wonders if Joey is still alive. She'd have to be twenty by now. She can't be—that would be a real stretch. His mother and Joey, curled on the couch, an Afghan around his mother's feet. He can see her eyes, lost in thought and alone. Few friends. As for family, just a few cousins—otherwise, an island.

He needs to get back to her. She called and gave him the news. Sean has been away for too long, neglected her, and the streak of remorse that bombards his stomach abrades him. He can feel it.

"It's a bobcat," the man says. "She's my first prize winner.

I'll show you the ribbon, have it right in the glove compartment."

Sean drops the viewfinder from his eye, hands it back to the man. The man forces a smile, as if he's drugged, snaps the ribbon out of the glove compartment and holds it up into the breeze. The blue ribbon snaps in the dark wind. The man also looks sleepy. For Sean this is all too much all at once. He prefers newness doled out.

"Taxidermist," he says, tapping his chest. "This is my best one. Doesn't she look *real*? I mean, like she could just reach out and chew on your neck. Raaaaaaaaawr!"

"Yes," Sean says. "I can see."

"You have a lot of stuff on your back. Do you need a ride somewhere?"

"Okay," Sean says. He knows better than to pass this one up, though this guy has something else underneath the surface and Sean has no interest in finding out what that is. "I'm heading south and also east. Arizona if you can get me there. Further east is good, too. I'm heading back to the other side."

"Good thing," the man says. "I am too. At least as far as south goes." The man tells Sean he's heading down to Bakersfield on business. He's down there to pick up some "critters." "Freelance work," he says. "Hop in," the man says. Taped on the dashboard is a picture of a large woman with heavy mascara. She has a beautiful smile, as if she has suffered and for once in her life is content. Sean keeps his backpack wedged between his knees. The man turns the ignition.

2.

In the jeep the man blasts Rachmaninoff but drives under the speed limit. The man tells Sean that Rachmaninoff is far more intense than heavy metal. He says he's not "into" classical music, just Rachmaninoff. "Listen to that pulse," he says. "That *beat.*" For an hour the man doesn't talk. He insists that they just listen so they do. Sean leans back in the seat and lets the stream of air flow over him. He closes his eyes. The animal stench in the car is heavy.

When one Rachmaninoff symphony ends, the man plays another one. When they pass Merced Sean can see the stars. Sean opens his bag, and digs around for one of the stale rolls. He can feel his stomach churn. Sean finds the bag of rolls and pulls one out. Some of the rolls have become flattened with the weight. He bites into one. It is as dry and tasteless as a cracker. He finds the sunflower seeds, and shakes some into his mouth. He doesn't look at the man. This is a conscious decision.

Once they pass Madera, the man says he has to take a piss. Sean can barely hear the man over the wind and the music, but Sean nods in compliance. The man pulls off onto the shoulder of Route 99 and stops the jeep. He walks down a slope and holds onto a tousled jacaranda and pisses down into the culvert. Sean watches the man's back, the wind catching his shirt. Sean looks behind the seats. The jeep is stacked with blue sealed plastic boxes. Sean remembers his mother used to keep his sweaters in these boxes. She took care of him, better than he thinks he deserved, in retrospect. Sean knows what is inside these boxes, but he's not sure he wants to see another dead animal. One stuffed animal a day is about all he can handle. The thrum of traffic whizzing by on the highway is steady, like static.

The man snaps the door open and plops behind the wheel. He bobbles his head and looks at Sean. He eyeballs Sean up and down.

"That felt good," the man says. Sean gets another whiff of the musky animal smell. Now Sean understands why the man drives with the top down. The man keeps staring. Sean wonders what this guy is thinking. He's not sure he wants to know that either. Nothing about this feels comfortable.

"Name's J.J., the man says. Forgot that somehow. Sorry."

"Sean."

"Nice to meet you, Sean," J.J. says. "That's a good name. Seaaaan." He closes his eyes, and sighs, puffing out his cheeks. He rubs his eyes with the back of his palms. Sean wants to ask if they are going to keep on going towards Bakersfield tonight, but he doesn't want to be rude. After all, he's the one getting a free ride. He thinks the man is trying to get Sean to ask him what's wrong. But Sean doesn't want to do that either. It's not his business.

"Do you see this picture?" J.J. asks. Sean nods. "Do you know who this is?" Sean shakes his head.

"This is my wife. Her name is Elva. I know, it's an unusual name. *Elva*. But then we're not exactly the usual couple. Regular freak show, right?" Sean notices that the wind has stopped. The air almost feels warmer, and the shadows of the trees are almost welcoming somehow. Sean wishes he had a hardboiled egg with salt and pepper. He wonders if he is protein deficient. He knows he probably is, he can feel it. He doesn't eat well and he should take care of himself. His mother would tell him that. She would help him.

"Elva grew up living in the mountains. She wasn't large then. That happened later. She lived so high up in the mountains that she could look down into the clouds. Her parents would drive down into the valley to go to the store, to visit society. Otherwise, she was inaccessible—cut off from everything. Later she told me she thought I was an extraterrestrial, or something close to that. Because of my, you know, skin. At any rate, the thing is she wanted to be loved in one place. She wanted me to take her to the top of some mountain and live with her, and love her, just the two of us. Just like her little family did it."

Sean can see where this one is going. Or he thinks he can. He puts his elbow on his knee and rests his chin on his fist. He thought about being cut off but Sean didn't want to strike up a connection with J.J. Not yet. He felt it was best to hold his cards.

"But that's not the way I wanted to live," J.J. says. He looks off into the shadows and clicks at his teeth with his tongue. "I still don't. I grew up on a ranch. I raised sheep. I rode horses. When I had to talk I talked about what I needed to do. I'm out here with you because I'm avoiding her. Know what I mean? I just can't stand being around people, including her. It's not personal. I love her, especially the idea of her. She's a good person and she loves me. But we can't be together, so we're doomed. The ranch is sold. Oh, and I'm a taxidermist of all things. And we live up near Paradise with nothing to do except drive each other nuts. Man, oh man. Things take a strange turn."

Sean doesn't know what to say. He's tempted to tell him about his own parents, about why he's heading east in the first place. He wants to talk about his mother and what is happening several thousand miles away. He thinks about going into his personal philosophy, but he knows he doesn't have a coherent one yet—at least not one that he can call his own. Sean watches the reeds shiver as the traffic passes. Sean also realizes he doesn't have much to offer this man in the empathy department. He is still trying to discover what that feels like closer to home.

"You want some sunflower seeds?" Sean asks.

The man shakes his head and squeezes a pressure point on his forehead.

"Well, at least you have her picture up. That's something." Sean decides to try.

"Shit," J.J. says. He says he has the picture up to remember her, to keep her in mind. Otherwise he'd literally forget what she looks like. Sean wants to tell him that he wouldn't. He wants to say that keeping her picture up is better than nothing at all. He wants to restore balance in some way—always difficult.

J.J. snorts. Rachmaninoff erupts from the speakers. "Forget it," J.J. shouts. He looks in the rearview and jerks the jeep back out onto Route 99. He drives fast, a notch or two faster than Sean would like.

3.

Driving down the San Juaquin Valley, J.J. does not utter a word. Sean watches him stare straight ahead. Sean watches his eyes. J.J. does not lift his eyes to the rearview or watch the other cars. J.J. looks straight down the dark road and drives. Sean drinks his water and closes the cap. It is dark.

Despite the roll and the seeds Sean is still hungry, but he's also concerned that he offended J.J. in some way. He wants to err on the side of saying nothing rather than saying the *wrong* thing. Sean knows not everybody is like this. He wonders if he should ask to see one of the other samples. Then again, Sean guesses he will never see J.J. again after tonight. In the long run it won't matter. But sometimes the smallest things do. Sometimes they add up and coalesce in ways you don't expect. This is life—a ribbon snapping blind and engulfed in darkness.

When J.J. exits into downtown Bakersfield, Sean feels as if he let the man down somehow. J.J. pulls into a shuttered bank parking lot, and pulls the emergency brake. The plywood covering the broken windows is scrawled with red and black graffiti. J.J. lifts his eyebrows and smiles. For a moment his face sparks alive.

"Here we are," J.J. says. Sean can hear a street sweeper churning its way over pavement. They are at the intersection of Truxton and Chester. Sean guesses it is probably midnight. Sean lifts his bag, and he's ready to reach into his wallet if he needs to. He knows he should offer J.J. ten dollars for gas, a token.

"Well, good luck with your business," Sean says. He opens the door to the jeep. He wants to say something, but what? He decides he better just let it go. The dry air is sharp with salt and grime. It reminds him of the beach. Sean bets it hasn't rained down here in months.

Sean can feel J.J. watching him.

"Hold on, kid," J.J. says. "Where are you sleeping?"

"I'm guessing they have a cemetery in here, or something," Sean says. "I'll find a quiet spot. I'm used to it, it's fine."

"Hold on, I can't let you sleep with the dead," J.J. says. "My fatherly side won't let me do it. I'm a father now—I have to look out for people."

Sean wants to ask him what he means by that, but he decides to let it go. Everything that needs to come out usually does. If J.J. wants to tell him, he will. J.J. eyes Sean from head to toe. He can tell J.J. doesn't approve, but then *he's* not hitching his way back home either. The downsides of this life are starting to come back to him. He didn't think about this when he sold the Tercel, but then again he didn't think of much then. J.J. seems as if he's weighing his decisions.

"Why don't you come crash at my sister's house?"

Sean starts to say that he thought J.J. was here on business, but J.J. waves him off. J.J. says that his sister happens to also live here, right down the road on Dracena. J.J. says he has a free place to stay, why not take him up on it? Sean thinks it over. J.J. doesn't seem shady exactly, not like some of the others. He has secrets, but Sean doesn't read malevolent intentions in his face, in his movements. Nothing like that at all. Sean is a good read, or he feels that he is.

If J.J. were younger Sean could see him even accompanying Sean on his trek back east—just something about him seems open to experience, ready for the road. The air is calm, an almost balmy wind wafting the squalid stench toward Sean. Then again the smell might be emanating from J.J.'s jeep. Either way, this corner of Bakersfield doesn't seem an appealing place to lay down for the night, and Sean might have to walk a mile or two to find one.

"Okay," Sean says. "I don't see why not."

"There you go," J.J. says. "Don't stare a gift horse in the mouth, right?"

Sean closes the jeep door, and leans back into his seat. J.J. says if Sean doesn't feel comfortable, he can always sleep in the backyard. Better that than a cemetery. But if that makes him feel more at home....

J.J. hits the ignition, takes a U-turn, and they angle down along the levee, and turn past concrete warehouses and storage facilities. The moving air feels good on Sean's face. Sean just wants to concentrate on that for now—the good feeling amongst the not-so-good.

4.

When J.J. knocks on the door the lights are off. A lightning-blue motorcycle sits in the driveway, but other than that Sean doesn't see or hear signs of life. J.J.'s sister's house is a small green bungalow. The front stoop is littered with a circle of four porcelain dwarves wearing various colored porcelain hats. One of the dwarves seems to be dancing. The others stand arms akimbo, smirking with menace. A tan garden hose drips into a bedraggled flower bed, several scrawny flowers poking up out of the sand. Three birdfeeders stand guard to the small spindly tree in the front yard—a tree which appears to be on its last legs. The walk is coursed with cracks and buckled.

J.J. taps on the window to the living room and he sniffs. Sean carries one of the blue plastic boxes, as J.J. requested. It is not heavy but he can feel something thudding around inside. J.J. wants to surprise her.

"She must be asleep." J.J. slides his hand into his back pocket and withdraws a single gold key. He partially opens the screen door and slides the key into the lock. Sean watches J.J.'s hands. J.J.'s fingers move with precision, never a wasted effort. The door clicks open and J.J. waves Sean into the house. Sean catches a whiff of bacon and he feels something smack into his shoulder. With the exception of the light from the front stoop, the house is dark. Sean can see a shadow moving against the back wall.

"Son of a bitch," a woman shouts, flicking an overhead light on. The woman is tall, rangy and muscular. She is wearing a leotard with a tight white sweater over it. Sean watches her neck muscles contract. Her curly reddish hair is pulled back in a ponytail.

She holds another shoe, seemingly ready to throw it, also. The woman sees Sean, drops her hold on the shoe to the laces. Sean sees two books with ripped spines on the mocha brown carpet. At least now he knows what hit him. Sean can hear a baby crying down the hall.

"Sorry, sorry, sorry," J.J. says. "I'm sorry, baby."

"Who the hell is *this*?" the woman says. J.J. shrugs, and gestures towards Sean.

"This is my new friend, Sean," J.J. says. "Sean, this is my sister."

"I have a *name*," she says. "You know that."

J.J. explains how he met Sean, when, and where. The woman leans back against the wall, ignoring the crying child. Her turquoise earrings sway and jingle lightly. She wears two clasped onyx bracelets, one on each wrist. Her skin seems barely stretched across her face, tight like the skin of a drum. Sean wonders if she has been dried out from the sun and air. J.J. explains he was held up—bad traffic and construction—that Sean can be his witness if she doesn't believe him.

"It's true. He was held up," Sean says. "We were held up. And then we got a flat, also." Sean doesn't understand why J.J. won't come clean when his sister is expecting him. Why lie? Sean wonders if J.J. was stalling somehow by picking him up, but for what purpose? The woman nods and smacks her lips. She doesn't seem to believe the story, but she drops the shoes, flips the lights in the kitchen and turns on the faucet. Sean can hear her filling glasses and clinking ice cubes into the glasses. J.J. mouths "thank you," and rolls his eyes. The woman carries three glasses on a wicker tray with red sashes. She places the tray on a coffee table, points for Sean to sit. J.J. take a glass and Sean places the plastic box under the coffee table, his backpack at his feet, and he sits on the corner of the sofa. J.J. sits across the room in a high-back maple chair with intricate geometrical designs along the top. The legs of the chair end in tree-like stumps, and each stump is wound with snakes and lizards and skinks. The chair looks like a throne, without the arms. Sean thumbs his heron necklace for comfort.

The woman pounds down the hall, and the cries shorten, then fade, then stop. She comes back, carrying a small car seat under her arm and the baby in the other. It looks precarious and Sean wants to offer to help. The woman doesn't resemble J.J. and Sean wonders if perhaps she is a half-sister, or a stepsister. Siblings simply don't look *that* different. She places the car seat on the coffee table and the baby in the car seat. The baby bobs his head at Sean. He has a muss of brown hair, and Sean thinks the baby could use a haircut. Looking at Sean seems to calm the baby. The baby grabs his toes and stares. A cat stretches himself on the mat in the kitchen, unfazed by the ruckus.

J.J. introduces his sister as Red Bark. He explains that she changed her name inspired by a reoccurring dream. Sean is curious about the dream and wants to ask her. He decides to wait. Her given Christian name of Florence never did it for her, she says. Nobody wants to be "Flo," she explains.

"Hey, I brought you something," J.J. says, pointing to the blue plastic box. Red Bark beams and mumbles that she was lonely without him. She says her life force feels drained. She says she feels like an empty casing.

"Just open the box, would ya? You know what it is already."

Red Bark does. She pulls out a stuffed calico kitten, then another, then another, then another. Five in all, each one on a small pine base. She arranges the stuffed kittens in a circle, as if they were each chasing the tail of the kitten in front. J.J. explains that she loved these kittens when they were alive, that she really loved them.

"What *happened* to them?" Sean asks. Red Bark touches a pressure point on her temple, as if the question is giving her a migraine. She waves the question off.

"We had to have them put under," J.J. said. "Too many kittens isn't healthy for a baby. All that dander and filth." Sean wonders if "we" means Red Bark. Is he covering for his sister's culpability? Red Bark squats next to the stuffed kittens and pets each one, one by one. She closes her eyes and winces in pain.

"They are perfect like this."

J.J. smiles. Red Bark removes her sweater, tossing it on the sofa next to Sean. Sean looks over the baby then at Red

Bark. She turns her back to Sean and faces J.J., and then approaches J.J. slowly, with a creeping motion. Sean watches her back as she moves. She has more muscles rippling in her back than Sean has in his entire body.

Red Bark sits on J.J.'s lap, on the throne, and suddenly begins licking his chin and cheeks, then his ears, and then he sticks out his own tongue. Sean doesn't know what to say or do so he looks away. He looks at the watercolor of Shiva. He looks at the small Amish quilt on the loveseat. He looks at the baby watching Red Bark and J.J. This is his sister? Or his "sister"?

"Do you want to watch? I bet you'd like to watch." Red Bark asks and then licks J.J.'s neck. "We could teach you a thing or two. It could be a tutorial." Red Bark and J.J. laugh. Sean doesn't laugh.

Sean stands up and sticks out his thumb for the baby and the baby grabs it. He wants to ask if they are related, but he doesn't. She rubs J.J.'s crotch. J.J. looks at Sean, and Sean squints. He shakes his head.

"It was a euphemism," J.J. says, closing his eyes. "She's my *spirit* sister, not blood. You think I would make out with my real sister? That's disgusting. Don't worry, you'll still have the back room." Red Bark slips the straps of her leotard off. They hang like handles at her waist. Again, why would J.J. feel the need to deceive him? What is happening here?

Sean remembers the first time he flew in an airplane. The feeling of lift-off stuck in his stomach for weeks. It was intoxicating and disturbing at the same time. There was something unnatural about it. One hundred years before not a single person had felt that, Sean thought, and now so many have—half of the world has experiences that the dead could only fantasize about. Sean would rather maintain his own garden. He thinks of his mother, her fingers in the loam. She was always planting daffodils or petunias or pruning the rose bushes. The dirt beneath her fingernails seemed permanent, ever-present. Hard worker, tough.

"I'm going to take the baby for a walk down the hall," Sean says. J.J. begins moaning, and Red Bark unlatches J.J.'s belt buckle. J.J. reaches out his arm, as if to tell Sean to stay put. Sean ignores him and lifts the baby and steps over the stuffed kittens. Sean carries the baby down the hall, pushing the last door on the right open. This room is stocked with mounds of junk—boxes of papers and magazines, plastic trash bags, toys, clothes everywhere. Sean doesn't see any furniture. Sean opens another door—bathroom.

Then he opens the door on the left, and finds the baby's room. The room is painted yellow with a swirling kaleidoscope mobile rotating above the baby's crib. Clothes are strewn all over the floor. Sean places the baby in the crib, and thankfully the baby doesn't cry. He can hear J.J. and Red Bark moaning in the living room. Sean closes the door, balls some of the baby clothes into a pillow case, and curls up under the crib. He presses clothes over his ears and he breathes through his nose. He hopes the sounds of his own breathing will drown out what he doesn't particularly want to hear. He has done this before. There could be worse things, Sean thinks. It's possible.

For some time Sean sleeps.

5.

When he wakes up, the room is still dark. Sean can hear the baby's raspy breathing above him. The room smells like sweat and baby shit. Moldering clothes. Sean tosses the pillowcase of clothes against the closet and lifts himself from the floor. He doesn't mind sleeping in his shoes, but he's had enough. Something about this place doesn't sit right with him. Sean doesn't like being lied to for no reason. Or for reasons that have yet to see the light.

At times like this Sean wishes he owned a watch. This is the opposite of everything he knew when he was young. He has no memory of being a baby or toddler, but he knows he was loved. And this baby? He's not so sure. It seems in the throes of abject neglect, despite the kitten holocaust he unwittingly inspired.

He creaks the door open and steps back out into the hallway. Sean can hear the sound of a fan oscillating and he can feel the wafting air. A wan light seeps in from the front porch. Red Bark and J.J. lay on their stomachs sprawled on the sofa bed, turned away from each other. Their bodies seem contorted, wracked in pain. Sheets and blankets and throw pillows twist around their legs. Sean can see that his backpack is underneath the sofa bed. Sean slides his feet as quietly as he can along the rug, and bends down to retrieve his backpack. The fan caresses his hair, wafts against his face. Sean understands. He likes sleeping with a fan in the background. He likes the white noise.

Watching Red Bark, Sean slips his hand under the foldout bed and grabs ahold of one of the backpack straps. When Sean tugs on the backpack, he can feel as if it is snagged on one of the supports for the mattress. He slides his other hand under the bed to free the backpack. Red Bark's eyes open. She stares at him. Sean whispers that he needs to get his backpack, but Red Bark just blinks. Sean tugs at the backpack again, then yanks harder. Red Bark lifts her torso, and with another tug Sean jerks the backpack free. He falls back onto the carpet.

Red Bark hisses at Sean, and Sean clenches his fists. She makes Sean nervous. She licks her lips. Red Bark lifts the sheet revealing her breasts. Her eyes look dreamy or drugged, or both.

"You want some?" She squeezes herself.

Sean stands up, slings the backpack on his shoulders. He likes the feel of the floor beneath his feet. Sean exhales, and runs his hands down his jacket. The solidness of it. He is quick and he knows what to do. Any inkling and he knows what to do.

"What's your baby's name?" Sean asks.

Red Bark stares at Sean as if she's possessed. Then she closes her eyes. Her eyes tumble underneath her lids. J.J. doesn't move. Sean can see the tuft of his hair and his neck.

"Gino," Red Bark whispers, dragging out the "ooooo." She sighs. "But I'm going to call him something else. Who knows? Do you have any ideas?" Then she widens her eyes. "What do *you* want to do right now? What do you *really* want to do?" Red Bark runs her hands up her stomach, and higher, cocks her head.

"How about Shooting Star?" It sounds right for him. Sean can still hear the congested breathing in the back of his mind.

Sean grabs at the doorknob, pushes the screen door open, and closes both quietly behind him. He breaks into a sprint, down the residential street and toward the water. His bag jostles, tugs at his shoulders.

Sean hustles along Truxton, past the brackish plains. He looks behind him, but he sees nothing. The undeveloped areas are littered with plastic bags, Coke bottles and beer bottles. The water smells fetid and polluted, and on the other side of the levee is a small canal. Sean can see the refineries and factories. He can imagine the oozing filth. Sean wonders what these plants *do* exactly. He wonders what the factories make, if anything. Or do they destroy? Sean wonders if it is worth it.

Sean can hear the distant howl of a train. The hoot lasts for several seconds, then drifts off. Sean can almost hear an echo. As a child Sean always lived near a train station. He feels a twinge of nostalgia, of loneliness. He thinks of his mother and how she would tell him the train is calling out for lost passengers, like the lowing of a cow.

He has always been this way. Sean resents these outside triggers. He'd rather jumpstart his own emotions.

From the darkness and the angle of the moon, Sean gauges that it must be around 4:00 in the morning. Sean is sleepy and he wants to rest and he knows that tomorrow he will have to find a new ride and knowing this makes him more tired. He'll have to try. He has to conserve his energy. Sean has to conserve everything—otherwise he'll never make it.

Only a few cars pass by on Truxton, and Sean isn't ready to start trying to find a ride. Sean wants to stay away from the banks of the levee, away from the sodden fields. The office buildings on the right might do. Sean crosses Truxton. He climbs an embankment and up into a series of parking lots. The lights from the buildings are enough to see by. In the rear of a small grey office building are two maroon Dumpsters, about three feet apart. Sean squeezes between the two Dumpsters, and leans against the concrete base of the building. He removes his backpack, takes a swig of warm water, eats another roll, and withdraws his small pillow. He folds the pillow in two and props it against the wall. This could be worse, Sean thinks. At least he has privacy. He is protected for the most part. Sean closes his eyes and crosses his arms. He falls asleep thinking of fans and trains and the calming sounds of them.

6.

Sean feels the fingers first. Then the thick grip of a hand on his clothes. "Hey, what are you *doing* here? Get the hell out of here." A fat man in a forest green dress shirt and a red tie stands over him. His face is flushed and piggy. The man kicks him in the thigh.

"I'm going. I'm going," Sean says. "Let me get my stuff."

"Yeah, get your shit and get the fuck out of here. You bum. I'm calling the cops right now." Sean wants to ask the pink-faced man if he knows of a good place to get a cheap breakfast, but he figures he better ask for restaurant tips elsewhere. The man kicks him again, then withdraws as if he suddenly realizes he might put *himself* in danger. The man opens an outside door and lets it slam behind him. Blinking in the sunlight, Sean hoists the backpack and scrambles down the slope.

A bum. Maybe that's all he is. He does feel unclean. He smells, he knows that. His hair is oily, scraggly and gritty with dirt. For now he does have the appearance of a bum. But then Sean would rather be a bum than live J.J.'s life. He doesn't want to be a confused lecher with a woman and a baby in a distant city and a picture of a sad, mistreated woman on the dashboard, one of many, seemingly. What's right is right, Sean thinks. No matter how poorly he stinks, Sean takes comfort in the fact that he doesn't damage anyone. At least not intentionally. He tries to do the right thing. Sean doesn't mind just disappearing—better that than injuring another. The feeling of being invisible is worth pursuing. Red Bark and J.J. understood this somehow. He would rather watch than involve himself. He'd rather keep two feet on the ground, stay rooted internally—keep a healthy distance from personal bedlam. And yet here he is wandering. His actions contradict his principles and he knows it.

Sean hikes across the train tracks and hurries across busy Route 99. The more he walks, the better he feels. Putting some distance between himself and the fetid canal is a goal worth shooting for in the short-term. He wants to save food, find some cheap eggs and waffles, some fat and protein—fill his stomach. Sean figures he can afford it, though he was prepared to dig through the maroon Dumpsters all morning if the suit didn't chase him away. Sean walks away from the industrial parks, through more residential neighborhoods, to the city streets. Most of the storefronts he sees are in Spanish. Tiendas. He asks an old man in a brown cardigan sweater where he might find breakfast. The man sweeps the sidewalk, but when Sean approaches he lifts his head and peals his sunglasses from his head. Sean realizes it must still be early.

"Desayuno?"

Sean nods. The Spanish word is so much more tempting

than "breakfast." It slides along the tongue.

"You go down to that corner," the man points with a knotty finger. "Go that way. You find."

Sean thanks him and is almost ready to give the man a tip. Sean can feel his stomach begin to eat away at itself. He feels weak, and knows he needs food quick. He is almost ready to abandon vegetarianism altogether, at least until he gets home.

Inside the Mexican diner, Sean orders fried eggs and beans and tortillas and a side order of orange juice. When his plate comes out, he slices the eggs quickly with his knife, and shovels them into his mouth. He nearly swallows the tortillas whole. The waitress turns away. She must be used to this, Sean thinks. He orders another plate, and the waitress says something to him in Spanish that Sean doesn't understand. Nobody wants to watch a starving man eat.

"No comprende," Sean says.

"I say you are a hungry little man," the waitress says, rubbing down the counter. She is short and squat, and her long hair reminds Sean of shoe polish. Her hair is tied back into itself, a tuft bobbing behind. The woman's apron is yellow with a purple border and a purple rooster emblazoned smack in the middle

"Tambien café por favor," Sean says.

"Si, claro," the waitress says. Sean watches her pour the coffee. It is dark coffee, just what he wants. Her forearms are taut and brawny and he can see the dark edges of tattoos underneath, on her shoulders. Sean guesses she has worked at the diner for some time. She might even be the owner, or the owner's wife. Sean doesn't know how to say owner in Spanish. He knows "jefe" means boss, but he's not sure if it would imply "owner" as well. He doesn't want confusion as a result of his limitations.

The waitress shuffles the cup of coffee onto a saucer and places it in front of Sean. Sean dumps sugar and milk into the coffee and drinks from the mug in rapid sips. It is sweet. She brings another plate of eggs and tortillas and black beans and hands Sean the handwritten bill on a small rectangle of paper. A group of Mexican men in jeans and sweatshirts sit at a table near the window. Another group sits closer to the counter. He looks away.

Sean eats the second plate as quickly as the first, and downs his coffee. He knows this will keep him going for most of the day. He will need more food later, but not for a while. The bill is only seven dollars and forty cents. Under the plate Sean slides a ten.

As Sean lifts his backpack and arranges it on his shoulders, the waitress smiles at him. She says something else in Spanish, but it is complicated and fast and Sean just nods and smiles. She smiles back and can tell he didn't understand.

"I say, good luck on your travels, little man. Where you going?"

"I'm heading home," Sean says. He doesn't say where that is. "I'll be heading home for a long time. Mi madre. Solamente." He misses his mother when he says this. He hopes he can get there in time.

The waitress says something else in Spanish and averts her eyes and she returns to wiping the counter. Sean can see the swish marks where she wiped, and the sun gleams in the wetness.

7.

After standing on the corner of Union and Bernard for three hours, Sean is exhausted. A few drivers slow down to stare. Otherwise, not a single nibble. He fills his water bottle from the grungy faucet in the men's room of the Taco Bell and he walks up Union. Sean is not hungry, but he's worn and he has trouble concentrating. His eyes burn. It could be worse, he thinks. The air is pleasant and dry. He has accessible food and money in his pocket—enough for now. Sean knows he is still at the beginning of things. Trouble lurks in the beginnings.

He finds a park with a small gray plaque reading "Central Park." Unlike the famous one, this park only stretches two city blocks. Men sit at dilapidated benches ringing the park. Some drink from paper bags. Some sit rocking back and forth. A few play chess and checkers. Sean sits on the sidewalk across from one of the chess matches and asks if he can have the next game. One man is fat, a bulbous golf-ball sized growth jutting from his temple. His eyes are watery, and he pulls his black Dodgers cap down over them. The other man is shorter with olive skin, and his hands are knobby and calloused. He looks to be of Eastern European descent—Hungarian? Romanian?—and Sean wonders if he speaks English. The eucalyptus tree filters dappled sun upon the two men. Sean doesn't see anyone in the park other than these men.

"Looks like we got us a challenger," the fat man says. He fingers his growth and laughs. The other bites his lip. A thin trickle of blood drips down onto his chin. Sean guesses that the man is from Greece. He leans back and gulps a quick drink from a paper bag. He wedges it back behind him, slashes his bishop across the board and takes the fat man's knight.

The fat man takes the bishop with his pawn. The Greek man sends his queen up the board, wedging it against a defended pawn. The fat man castles. Sean watches the action, sipping his water and screwing the top closed. Sean reaches into his backpack and pours sunflower seeds into his mouth. They taste salty and good. He offers some to the men, and the fat man sticks out his hand. When the fat man wins he tells the Greek that it's his turn to sit on the sidewalk and watch. Sean leans his backpack against the bench and sits.

Starting out, Sean does well. Playing black, he keeps his eyes on the board, trying not to allow himself to become distracted by the growth. He castles, stays defensive. He stays back, fending off the fat man's advances with his pawns and bishops. Sean allows his knights to emerge, to keep the fat man's bishops at bay. It works for about ten moves, until the fat man surprises Sean by sacrificing his King's bishop to blow open a hole in Sean's defense. Fifteen moves later and the fat man has five pieces trained on Sean's king. Sean allows himself a drink of water before he loses. Then he loses. Sean shrugs, pretending to be nonchalant. Inside he smolders.

"Good game, kid," the fat man says. He laughs and the Greek bites his lip again. The line of blood has dried on the Greek's chin. "Keep practicing." He asks both men if they know where he might hitch a ride. He tells them he's heading east. The fat man coughs and fingers his growth. He spits into the patch of weeds behind the bench and hocks his throat.

"Go down to the river," the fat man says. "The GPI building. They're always heading out, usually down to San Diego on delivery." Sean tells the fat man he's not riding in a truck. "Should have luck there."

"I've had bad experiences," Sean says.

"Beggars can't be fucking choosers, can they?"

"No," Sean says. "But I'd prefer to ride in a car."

"These are vans, kid. So just relax wouldja? It's just a bigger car."

Sean thinks about it and thanks the man and lifts his backpack. The Greek makes kissing noises at Sean and takes another gulp from his paper bag. Sean decides to ignore this, though he's tempted to knock out the guy's teeth. He'd rather whoop him in chess.

Sean just takes it and walks on away from the park, back up towards the levee. The sky looks darker towards the west. Sean doubts it will rain, but it's possible. The wind picks up. He tightens the straps on his backpack and trudges forward.

8.

After hiking up and down Truxton, Sean finally finds the small dusty GPI building. The vans in the parking lot give it away. He raps on the dented metallic front door, knowing you can't be *too* shy and get anywhere. He also knows if this doesn't work he will have to hike up the ramp to 99 and start making his way out of town, one way or another. When the door finally opens, Sean stares at a woman in a blue button-down uniform with a plug of chaw under her lip. Her hair hangs in clumpy braids. One of her eyes is brown. The other is blue. Her teeth are the color of overripe pineapple. She spits off to the left.

"Yeah? Whatchu want?"

Sean knows he has nothing to be nervous about, but he's starting to feel antsy. He needs to be back on the road. He has a destination. Sean wants to at least be working toward this, making progress. Sean tells the woman about the man in the park, about the tip. The woman bobs her head, looking Sean up and down.

"You got cash?"

"Yeah," Sean says. "But I can take a bus with cash. I heard I might be able to bum a ride. I can only offer a little bit."

"How much?" She spits near Sean's feet again.

"Depends on where you are headed," Sean says. He thinks this is honest. Sean can see this woman is out for herself. She's about the bottom line.

"Depends on what you want to ante up is what I'm saying. But you got five seconds, then I'm back to business."

"All right. Five bucks to Arizona."

"We're not going to Arizona today. Seven bucks to San Diego."

Sean doesn't know what to do. He needs to go east, not south. San Diego is not a help—there he's no closer to home than when he started. Sean knows the key to hitching is connecting the dots. Go from one connection to another—keep moving in the right direction. But Sean doesn't see how this is good news.

"That's okay," Sean says, and strums his backpack straps. He'd rather hoof it, rather go at it alone. He's halfway across the parking lot when the woman barks out to him: "Hey, how about out to Barstow? Five bucks." Sean nods, and backtracks. He pulls out five wrinkled ones and she counts them out. The wind blows the fetid smell of the levee up the slope. The woman lifts her eyebrows.

"Hop in," the woman says, pointing to a van at the back of the lot. "It's unlocked." The woman sniffs and spits against the side of the GPI building. Sean nods and says he'll just wait for the driver. He sits on the curb.

"That's fine," the woman says. "But you're looking at her. And I'll be ready in five." She closes the door behind her, locks it. Looking out over the levee, Sean watches the darkness encroach upon the blue. He can see it all unfold in front of him. Another train blares. Sean wonders if J.J. and Red Bark are still going at it. He wonders if J.J.'s wife knows or if he has a wife at all. He wonders if J.J. has any other Red Barks on the side in other California towns. Sean shakes his head, dazzled at the pointless muddle.

He realizes he hasn't seen an animal since he's been in town. J.J. would starve if he had to do business in town. Good think he has a wife who likes to live in the mountains, Sean thinks.

The woman leads Sean to the van and she tells Sean he can throw his backpack in the back. Sean's surprised by this, since he guessed the van would be stuffed with whatever it is GPI delivers. When the woman throws the doors open, the back is empty with the exception of six men sitting on the floor of the van. They look at the ground. The windows of the van are tinted.

"Throw your bag in there," the woman says. Sean says he'd rather keep it up front. The woman shrugs, and slams the door closed. "Don't blame you," she says. The woman turns the ignition and Sean squeezes his backpack at his feet. The front of the van is sealed off from the rear with a black grate. It's as if they are in a prison transportation vehicle.

Sean doesn't say a word. He doesn't tell this woman his name and he's not about to. He doesn't want to know what hers is either. The woman spits into a Styrofoam cup, and she places it in the cup holder. The woman drives west through the city and out into the darkening clouds. She hits Route 58 at ninety miles per hour, and the dust flumes around them.

"Bakersfield is a toilet," the woman says. She opens the glove compartment. Inside Sean sees a gun in a holster. "Isn't it?"

Sean shrugs.

"People come in to take a piss on their way to LA or Vegas. I'm always glad to get the hell out of this dump."

Sean interlocks his fingers and picks at his nails. He can feel the woman watching him. He wishes he were in the back with the others. There is safety in numbers, he thinks. Camaraderie, unspoken. Whispers of Spanish behind him. Dark, faces—chiseled.

He closes his eyes. The Afghan over her feet. A soft spot on the sofa where the cat used to sleep, some small hairs still in evidence. She holds her stomach. She closes her eyes. Her hand reaches out into the void.

9.

Sean leans his head against the window, but the van jostles. The view from the window is desiccated—browns and grubby yellows. Sean is drawn to the desert, but not this desert. Sean wants to ask her where she is taking these guys. For a moment he wishes he could play investigative reporter, expose the truth. But he knows his position is precarious at best. He has to think about that.

The woman reminds him of girls in high school, the kind that have it out for everyone. The woman holds her head, arches her neck. Yeah, Sean thinks, there is something disdainful about her. This woman would stab her own mother in the gut if it would advance her own cause in the world.

The road climbs and they cross the nubs of the El Paso Mountains. They pass signs for Caliente and Tehachapi, and they burn over the Los Angeles Aqueduct and pass through the town of Mojave. As they approach Edwards Air Force Base, one of the men in back clambers for "el baño," "el baño." Finally he says "rest stop por favor! Rest stop!"

There is a blanched sign. The arrow points to the right, east.

"No rest stop," the woman says. She winces and withdraws her cell phone from a niche in the dashboard. "No baño. No baño."

The Mexicans grumble "puta," but the woman doesn't acknowledge it. The woman says something in Spanish, something about "una hora mas." This desert is so ugly and colorless, Sean thinks. He wants to like it but he feels agitated. Sean finds it difficult to keep his eyes open.

They pass Four Corners and Hinkley and enter Barstow. They pull off 58 onto a side road and onto another side road.

"You can drop me here," Sean says. "Don't want to have to walk all the way back into town."

"You don't, huh?" The woman stares straight ahead and keeps driving.

"No, you can drop me here," Sean says. Sean guesses they have already driven a mile from town.

"Can I?" She speeds up. She keeps driving.

Sean shakes his head. He should have trusted his intuition. He should have realized that this was trouble. This woman and this situation.

The woman keeps driving, faster. There is nothing Sean can do. The woman drives down a dirt road, and then takes another dirt road from that. Sean can see the air still thick with smog from L.A. and dust intermixing with it. Maybe rain? But that seems unrealistic. Sean is beginning to feel nervous. He doesn't like the games. The gun. The cell phone. The surreptitious nature of this whole trip.

"Let me out of this van," Sean states. "I want to get out." The woman glares at him, and Sean is tempted to pull the gun out of the glove compartment. He'd like to see how tough she is then. Instead, she speeds up, then slams on the brakes. The Mexicans crash into the screen and cuss. Sean braces himself with his hands.

"Get the fuck out then," she says. "With your whining." She doesn't look at him. She is not trustworthy. She is not someone he wants in his presence. Sean would rather hike through the desert, chewing on his arm. "I *was* going to be nice to you, but I guess that's not what you want."

"No, I want to get out," he says.

Sean pushes the door open, and the Mexicans bang on the van. Sean doesn't want to see any more. He didn't want any more knowledge of this operation, whatever it is. He slams the door and bolts down the road in the opposite direction. The van lurches forward, and the dust and gravel kicks in his direction.

He's at least three or four miles from town, and with no cars in sight Sean knows he's going to have to get a move on.

He puts one foot in front of the other. He has food. He has a pint of water, though Sean knows he will need much more soon. And out here the temperatures will drop quickly. Sean guesses it is already at least three. He takes a quick sip from his water and picks up the pace. At least he has water. Dry lightning spiders up ahead and the sky is darker.

10.

Sean walks. Then he walks some more. He watches: left foot then right foot. Right foot then left foot. His shoes are worn. He can feel the hump of each pebble beneath his feet. A pickup truck passes now and then, but Sean can't even see the faces through the gray dust. Nobody stops. He is down to the dregs of his water. This is the only emergency.

The light pales. Sean can barely see his own feet. He can see the lights of the town off in the distance, but he doesn't have the energy. And even if he makes it there, where will he sleep? He would have to find a Dumpster, a hidden corner. Might as well find a place out in the bushes, he thinks. It will be as cold here as it will be there. The clouds still loom, but nothing happens. Either way this is some kind of blessing, Sean thinks. If it rains, he's soaked, but he can collect water. If it doesn't, he's dry but thirsty. It never rains here—maybe someone is looking after him.

The scrub and ocotillo doesn't seem appealing, especially in the dark. He leans against the scrub. The thorns rake his jacket, jab him. He trips over rocks. He scuffs in the sand for a sandier place, a softer spot, something away from the road. He especially doesn't want the smuggling crews to spot him. Sean just hopes he doesn't end up sleeping on top of a snake hole, over the den of some animal. Sean can hear a truck rumble down the dirt road, but when he looks up he can't see the truck. It must be miles away.

Sean walks down into an arroyo and up the other side. There, well behind two ocotillo, Sean finds a sandy swath and he kicks the few small rocks from the spot. Drops his pack. On his knees he picks pebbles and thorns, and tosses them down into the arroyo. He sits in the sandy bed, and opens his pack. He takes out a sweatshirt and puts that on top of his jacket. At least that will cover up my own stink, he thinks. Now he wonders what he was thinking when he packed. He packed too light. No winter coat, not enough clothes. I will pay for it out here, he thinks. He's already cold.

Sean feels for his Sterno and tugs it from the tangle. He finds the can opener and a can of something. He opens the can, though it's too dark to tell what the can contains. Probably better that way. He drinks the bean water in one gulp. Sean pries open the fuel can, finds his matches and he lights the Sterno fuel. The can will do just fine, Sean figures. He finds his fork and places the can directly over the heat. He stirs it as the fire warms. What to do about water? This is his only thought.

When the beans are done he eats them right from the can, slides the lid back on the fuel. Not enough water even for coffee, Sean knows. He dips the last of the hard rolls into the bean juice and eats them like that. When the bread is gone he uses his fork, then his fingers to scoop out what coats the inside of the can. He licks the inner ridges of the can, what he can reach with his tongue. There is water in these beans, he thinks. If he has to, Sean knows he will drink the bean water, the corn water. That's something. He eats some peanuts, but they are too salty for now. Sean feels his stomach digesting its own lining, but there's not much he can do about it. His throat is dry.

When he is done, Sean wraps himself in the army blanket. Uses it as a mummy wrap. Then he slides himself into the sleeping bag. Sean wonders how cold it will get, but decides not to think about that. He is tired but he isn't sleepy. He knows he won't be able to fall asleep right away, but he doesn't have a choice about that either. The sand cools and Sean shivers, curls himself into a ball. He knows it will only be ten or eleven hours. He can make it that long.

Eventually Sean drifts off, though the cold wakes him. He pulls another sweatshirt on and places socks on his hands and sweatpants over his pants. He wraps a shirt around his ears and nose and rewraps himself in the blanket and the sleeping bag. There is nothing he can do but shiver and wait it out.

It is still dark when the rain starts. The sound of thunder wakes him. Thunder without lighting. Then the rain comes. Sean knows the bean can is already open, but he throws off his blanket and digs through the bag for containers. He lays out everything he can—the few pots and pans, the water bottle. He digs the matches under his pants, in his underwear. He knows the wetness won't help him sleep better, but for a moment he smiles, knowing at least he will be able to make coffee in the morning. He will have water. The rain falls. The rain soaks. He goes back to shivering in the sand, the now-wet sand.

11.

When the sun rises through the haze, it is a beacon of deliverance. Sean lifts his head to it and basks. He sits on a rock and he concentrates on warming. He thinks of warmth. Sean does jumping jacks to warm himself. He is soaked and his sleeping bag and blanket are soaked. The inner contents of his backpack should be fine, he knows.

After an hour Sean is drier and warmer. He examines his water supply. The containers caught some water, but not as much as he hoped. He pours what he collected into his water bottle. He drinks some of it and feels better. The water tastes like beans still, but he doesn't mind. It is wet and cold. When he is warmer Sean walks up and down the arroyo, searching for puddles. The sand is wet, but the water has drilled through the sand. He finds some water puddles on flat rocks. He trickles this water into his cooking pan, and then trickles that into his water bottle. Soon Sean knows the water will evaporate. Sean hurries to find water.

Sean drinks more water. Sean has enough to boil and make some coffee, and he does. The coffee tastes bitter, but it gives him energy. Sean knows he will need the energy to make it to town with the sun beating upon him. He will save the rest for his trip. He eats more sunflower seeds and a mealy apple. There is water in that, he knows—even if only a bit. He wrings out his sleeping bag and his blanket the best he can. He wraps both around his neck, pulls his backpack on. He knows they will dry in the sun this way.

As Sean walks, he twists the sleeping bag and blanket to

expose them to the sun. He can feel them drying, though Sean knows they will make him sweat. The landscape is monotonous and dusty. Gray sand. Ocotillo. Rocks. Brush. Sean sips his water carefully, saving each drop. Cars pass on the dirt road more frequently, and Sean can see billboards ahead in the distance and buildings. Sean eats some raisins and walks on. Right then left. Left then right.

When Sean reaches the adobe building, a girl with green horseshoe earrings sits behind a glass-paned wall, drinking coffee from a tall white mug. She stares at Sean, and Sean asks for the bathroom. The girl points around the corner and her eyes follow him. Sean can hear the sounds of children playing inside. Sean is grateful for the lock; he locks the bathroom behind him. He takes a long drink from the faucet. He drinks until he can feel his stomach filled with water and then he drinks some more.

He takes off his jacket and sweatshirt and shirt and runs the hot water. He soaks paper towels in the hot water and dabs his face and neck and chest with them. He soaks more paper towels and dabs his arms, and under his arms. He splashes his hair with water and dries it with the paper towels. He leans over the sink and drinks the water. He turns the hand drier on his face, and wonders if he has enough time to dry his blanket and sleeping bag this way.

When Sean puts his clothes back on, someone knocks at the door.

"You need to come out of there now," a woman's voice says. It doesn't sound like the voice of the girl.

"Okay," Sean says. He pulls his jacket on, gathers his backpack. He unlocks the door.

When he walks out a large woman with a broom in her hand stands in front of the door. Her face is speckled with freckles or dirt or both. He thinks of J.J.'s wife. If she even exists.

"You need to leave," she says. "We don't have room for stinking roustabouts."

Sean doesn't say a word. He walks around the corner and through the corridor and out the door.

12.

Sean walks down the sandy Barstow main street. The sidewalk seems to evaporate in the dry air. The grey brows of the Mojave ridges make the street seem insubstantial. East Main Street is littered with signs for ghost town tours. That must be a life, he thinks—giving those tours. Sean walks towards the sounds of a train. The spaciousness is disorienting.

At the 7-11 Sean buys more raisins and peanuts and chocolate, and a package of wheat bread. He buys three bananas, though they are a dollar each. He buys two large containers of water, though he doesn't know how he will carry them. He figures he's thirsty enough to drink at least one in the next hour. He starts drinking.

The man behind the counter looks Sean up and down, and Sean asks him if he knows where he might find a ride out of town. The bearded man wears glasses too large for his face and his teeth are yellow, and the man's forehead is speckled with acne. The man hocks his throat and doesn't answer and Sean sees that he has some greenish debris in his beard. Sean wonders if he knows or just doesn't care. The man takes Sean's money and hands him wrinkled change.

Sean on the curb outside of the 7-11. He eats bread and one of the bananas and two squares of the chocolate and watches the cars park and people walk into the 7-11. He hopes he can find a ride this way. Sean hates sticking his thumb out, like some 1930's vagabond. He thinks of himself as a passenger more than a hitchhiker. But he feels grimy and tired. But the sun is warm on Sean's back. He can hear the trucks on the interstate. The passersby wear sunglasses, and don't answer when Sean asks for a ride. Sean wishes he had a phone—it is one of those times.

The sun drifts behind the storefront, and Sean sits in the shade. He asks a woman carrying her dog for a ride. She doesn't look at him. Sean asks three men in a shiny purple SUV. They have long hair and bandanas and bikes on their bike rack. They say: "sorry, man." Sean asks a guy driving a rusted bronze Cadillac. The man shakes his head and comes out drinking a tall bubbling soda.

Sean finds a place against the building. He leans against the structure of the 7-11 and closes his eyes. He thinks of his mother. He can hear the muffled shouting. His father mostly. A door slams shut, more yelling. The desperate sounds of scratching, scrabbling, then more yelling. Eventually a door opens, and then slams shut. Feet thumping down the stairs. Arms crossed, Sean drifts off. He knows he should call. He can picture her, eyes closed, hands clasped over her chest as if she is deceased. She is not deceased—not yet. She has time; he can feel this.

The point in his side wakes Sean up. He turns his head and the man from behind the counter pokes Sean with a broom handle.

"Hey, you can't stay here," the man says, spitting against the wall near Sean. "You need to move. No fucking loitering you piecea shit."

Sean lifts himself, and holds his head in his hands. Here he is, still in California. He needs to find a way home, but he is finding it much more difficult than he imagined. Much more difficult than it used to be.

"I'm just trying to find a ride," Sean says. He pulls his fingers through his hair and smells them. They smell like rotten eggs. He wants a shower and a bed. He knows he can't afford a motel, but maybe somewhere he can find these things. For this to happen Sean knows luck will have to grace him.

"Fine. But you can't just plop down here." The man flips the broom around and sweeps cigarette butts into the drain. People and their brooms. "Tell you what," the man says. "Let me ask our candy guy."

Sean squints through the sun. An orange van sits in the handicapped spot with its blinkers flashing. The rims of the van are stained with a reddish dust. The blinks click. Sean can hear the rigs rumbling on the interstate. He hopes it doesn't come to this. Inside the store Sean can see the bearded man talking to a tall man in a red and white uniform. The man in the uniform looks like a candy cane, or a lost member of a barbershop quartet. Sean closes his eyes and crosses his fingers. Luck is usually not on his side.

The candy man steps out into the sun and tips his cap.

"I understand you are in need of transportation," the man says. The man adjusts his bow tie. He smooths his thin mustache with his thumb and index finger. His bow tie is yellow and green with a hint of pink. Candy cane?

13.

The man holds the door open for Sean, asks him to sit in the back seat. Very courteous. The front seat is loaded with stacked white boxes. Sean thinks of J.J. the taxidermist. Blue boxes. White boxes. Everything is sealed and delivered, Sean thinks. The inside of the van smells like burnt sugar, cardboard, and pineapple. Much better than rotting fur. Sean can imagine worse.

Sean has the far right corner of the back seat to himself. The rest is occupied with crates of shrink-wrapped candy and more white boxes. Wedging his backpack between his knees, Sean leans his head back against the seat. He hopes the candy man doesn't want to talk. He really doesn't feel like talking and can't bear the thought of starting all over again. Sean's feels his energy seeping from him slowly, a bit less of it each day.

The candy man primly slides behind the wheel of the orange van. He smiles rows of perfect white teeth. The top of the man's head nearly touches the ceiling of the van. He sits stiff and rigid, and he turns his head to look at Sean.

"Are you prepared for takeoff?"

"Yeah," Sean says, squinting through exhaustion.

"I know you may lack requisite room for stretching and relaxation, but please, at least put your mind at ease," the man says. "Half of the battle is perception." The man's formality strikes Sean as odd. It doesn't fit the dumpy surroundings. The man turns the ignition, and a blaring electric guitar blasts through the muffled speakers. He thinks of J.J. and his Rachmaninoff. Nothing matches. Sean closes his eyes, and leans his head against the window. Despite the music, Sean sleeps.

In his dream Sean stands over an expanse of asphalt. A man throws a red box in front of him. When Sean bends to pick up the red box, the man withdraws a gun and shoots Sean in the temple. Sean wakes up, his heart hammering in his jacket. He realizes this is just a dream and that he's on his way. The candy man drives. The landscape spools by. He goes back to sleep. He sleeps a long time. Sean is on his way now, he can feel that. He's heading home.

His mother needs him, she said. She said the word "need." Badly, he knows this—though she would never say it. And in a few more days he will be there. That is the reason, the only reason, he knows. The only reason he can think of to put himself on the road. The glass in the road glints, catches long fingers of sun. Some of the fingers seem to touch his forehead. Luck is on his side for a safe passage, he thinks. And he will do the right thing until he cannot any longer. He does not know when that will be. At some point the clouds will conceal the light and then he will have to start all over again.

Sean does not believe, but he kneels on the floor of the car. He closes his eyes, presses his hands together. Let her be okay, he whispers. You can take me. Let her be okay. That is all I want.

A Beach Tale

Friday

Donnie doesn't want a haircut. For the past two years he has permitted his hair to amble down his back, between his shoulder blades, and why change now? Donnie's hair isn't greasy or unkempt. When he needs to look presentable he squelches into a taut ponytail—slicked, combed, and business-like. But usually he lets it flow in one broad mane. Donnie's hair has been this way for so long. His mother's request feels like a betrayal.

Donnie sighs and pulls his car into the strip mall parking lot. He parks in front of the barbershop. Inside two customers flip through magazines. He wonders if he should back out, tell his mother the barbershop was too crowded—another time. Tell Mom he'd get his haircut after the trip. Nah, he thinks. Not worth the explanation, not worth the crouched posture he'd have to strike. He decides to just go for it. A new me, he thinks.

The light filtering through the cirrus cloud cover is a wan ocher, the color of melted Styrofoam. Pollution. Pretty soon sunsets will be purple, Donnie thinks. Then what? Then what?

But what does it mean to go for it? Donnie sits in his beige Taurus listening to the motor idle. His hands flutter. He sighs. He feels preposterous. He knows he's working himself up over nothing, but it is past time for going back now. It's just hair, Donnie thinks. I can grow more. Later. Then he begins combating himself: if it's just hair, then why does it matter to me? If it's just hair, then why do we have whole industries that survive on nothing more but a few snips of scissors? I should care because this is a statement of myself, because this is part of who I am as an American, he thinks. Why not lop off an arm while you're at it? It's just an arm. Identity is for idiots, Donnie thinks. But still...

A woman carrying two large paper bags toddles in front of Donnie's vision to the left, making her way to her minivan. He notices flaps of skin dangling from her arms. Her legs strain against the fabric of her margarine-yellow shorts. Her eyes seem withdrawn in some kind of shame. She watches her feet as she walks. Her hair is dyed a gauche bronze the color of the aluminum wrapping on chocolate coins. Her eyes wilt from the weight of her mascara. She bleeps her door unlocked, and bends down to plop the bags on the floor of the vehicle.

Donnie feels sorry for her, though he knows he shouldn't. He feels sorry for lots of people, a tendency he's trying to work on. Pity is patronizing, Donnie thinks, a weakness. Still, this woman is an especially sad sight to behold—she feels sorry for herself, also. She must receive blunt mockery every day of her life and behind-the-back comments must trail her every move. Donnie closes his eyes for a moment. He can feel her humiliation throbbing. It emanates from her—a purple glow. He's glad to have *his* set of problems rather than hers. Then he feels guilty for entertaining that thought. Jesus.

Stepping out of the car, Donnie throws his lanky shadow across the parking lot, stretching to the sidewalk leading up to the barbershop. His face is lucid and open to suggestion, but his skeptical eyebrows betray the contradiction: he looks older than he is. His skin looks wrung-out and worn, and his hair sometimes seems tinged with gray, though it's not. It's just the sheen, the gloss.

Donnie's arms and legs are freckled with small surface welts—he picks his skin when he's nervous. Habits die hard, as the chestnut goes. His clothes look generic—medium length black shorts and a plain white T-shirt. This is a guy who likes to blend in. Yet, it's difficult for him to tell if he's a man at all or still just a boy in the midst of a late bloom. He's on the verge. Donnie walks through the shadows huddling against the window of the barbershop. He scuffs quickly on the entrance mat.

Donnie's mother asked him to get a haircut—the whole family is traveling to the beach for vacation this afternoon, and she doesn't want to be disgraced by his "hippie hair." At breakfast she said, "I usually don't mind, honey, but when it's all of us that's different. This is just hair we're talking about. Plus, there's your father." Donnie didn't object—he rarely does. He nodded and took her comments as a matter-of-fact. Donnie lives at home with his parents. "Still?" his few friends ask when they decide to call him up, or get together for a brainless film, or for a few beers, or to play pool. He usually shrugs.

Donnie has never been in a hurry to do much of anything, yet he knows he's intelligent and that he will succeed. "I'm just on different time-scale," he says in his own defense. He's twenty-three and he attends the local community college. He does odd jobs around the neighborhood for extra money. Recently he's trimmed shrubs in the neighborhood park. That's the kind of job he likes. Short. No major obligation. No red tape. No thinking. Only doing. Clipping and breathing.

Partially hunched, Donnie walks through the doors with an air—as if he's entering a museum, or a chapel. He sits next to a ruddy-faced man flipping through an issue of *Cosmo* with his fingers running along the spine. Donnie can smell the syrupy lilac perfume pouring from the magazine. He sits with his knees together like a schoolgirl and stares straight ahead at the empty hangers of the coat rack swaying gently in the air-conditioned breeze. He listens to the light jazz twinkling through the overhead speakers. Waiting is something Donnie never minds doing. He can always ruminate.

I wonder what Janet wants to talk about, Donnie wonders. I wonder what she wants. Whatever it is, it can't be good. He knows this much.

When Carl waves and points to his chair, Donnie walks delicately, as if he might break a piece of furniture or shatter the storefront glass. Donnie feels particularly sensitive today, though it must be more than the haircut. Carl drapes the apron over Donnie and fastens it around Donnie's neck. Donnie tells Carl he wants a buzz cut. Carl's eyebrows rise. In the mirror Donnie notices a mole slightly below Carl's right eyebrow. He's never noticed that before. This is a whole new Carl, he thinks. Donnie's conception of Carl is completely different now: he's an eyebrow-mole man, more European somehow, or something. More urbane.

"You sure?"

"Sure," he says.

"Okay because we can't exactly glue it on after we're done. Catch my drift?" Donnie nods.

Donnie doesn't notice Carl's scissors lowering. He's thinking about elementary school. He's always been fixated on moles, but in elementary school he went so far as to cover the moles on his chest with Band-Aids. This started after a shirts and skins game of basketball. The girls pointed at the assortment of brown blotches on his chest, sniggering to themselves and turning away in a cluster of whispers. He started noticing how many moles he had. When he was ten he counted thirty-nine moles, and that didn't include the larger freckles.

Donnie started reading about moles. He read that most people have, on average, fifteen to twenty moles, but that some people have as many as one hundred moles. He began to wonder what the world record was for number of moles on a human body, though he never found out. Donnie and his friend Damon tried to pick each other's moles off using their fingernails. They became frightened though when blood oozed under the marred blemishes.

What was it about moles that created such an obsession? Donnie knew he was a fierce perfectionist, that he always hated mistakes. Perhaps that was it. Little evil brown spots. But he saw pictures of Marilyn Monroe, and she was considered one of the most beautiful women during her time. Her iconic beauty mark. He noticed people in everyday life that had enormous moles on their face, or neck or arms, and they seemed successful, unblemished internally.

He liked the way moles marked the skin. They create character, Donnie thinks. He liked the variety—the different colors: pink, tan, reddish brown, dark brown, black; he liked the different shapes and the way moles surprised you by appearing in the strangest unexpected spots. They're like insects, Donnie thought—they're everywhere, but often unobserved.

Then there were the really odd moles—the large protruding ones, the ones that shot forth hairs like a desert cactus, the ones resembling faces or animals or geometrical shapes. Skin-colored raised moles. One kid he knew had moles in his armpits. Another kid had them under his hair. He used to be repelled by women who had them. In elementary school he used to call one girl "mole neck" as a result of the moles that speckled her throat. Now moles fascinate him, and he likes women even more if they have a few readily visible. A mole remarks on a section of flesh, Donnie thinks.

I haven't been to the beach for years, Donnie thinks. I bet I'll have all kinds of moles to inspect then. Not that it will make it any better—it's still the boring beach. After one day he knows he'll find himself mired in a dreary funk, unsure what to do, bored, and claustrophobic. Carl flips the electric clippers on and dabs Donnie's side-burns. Donnie notices himself in the mirror. His hair is cut close to the skull. He feels as if he is seeing his face for the first time. He looks down at his black ponytail curled at his feet, like a scarf, like a tail, like some lost appendage.

This is different, Donnie thinks. This is strange. I wonder what Janet will think.

The schmaltzy jazz is beginning to get to Donnie. It sounds tinny and bubbly and overly upbeat—as if it's trying to sell him something. He's ready to go. Anyway, he is supposed to be at the hill by two. Just then he realizes he forgot his watch. In fact, Donnie can't remember where he put it at all. Good thing the haircut is over. Donnie asks Carl for the time. "One ten," he says.

Donnie looks out the window. The young saplings blow lightly in the balmy wind. The sunshine washes over the buttery sidewalk. The streetlights reflect the glare. A mother walks from her car holding her son's hand. Everything is perfect, like a model of itself. Donnie pays for the haircut, tipping Carl two dollars, and he steps out into the world.

Donnie guesses it is one forty, though he doesn't know for sure. The angle of the sun is certainly past twelve, slightly cockeyed towards the west. Donnie stands on the top of the place he simply calls "the hill." It's one of the highest spots in the county—the highest that he knows of at least. The hill is Donnie's thinking place, where he goes to reflect and process his thoughts. Nobody else knows about it except Janet. If anybody else is aware of the hill, Donnie has never seen them.

The hill is treeless at the top, though it is fringed with spruce knobs. From above Donnie imagines the hill looks like a monk's head. To the west Donnie can see splotches of farmland along the river, though now newer tract mansions line the waterfront. The park stretches to the north—more spruce trees, and pine trees, and deciduous arbors rolling towards Pennsylvania. To the east, expansive constellations of housing developments stretch as far as the horizon. The land is flat in that direction, on a slope to the city and the bay. To the south, more of the same; only in addition to the houses, Donnie can pick out the strip mall parking lots, the clothing stores, the grocery stores, the gyms and the banks.

He wonders about Janet's loyalty. Not that he's cautiously jealous. What's the point? But Donnie has heard rumors that Janet's been out with this guy or that guy. He's dated her for a year and a half, but he can't help but wonder. Does she love him? Does she truly see herself with him in the long run? He has his doubts. If it doesn't work out with her he won't be angry. He won't be distraught. He won't. But he feels a magnetic tug of some kind. Perhaps habit? Donnie doesn't know why he feels this way—and maybe she's picked up on that. Maybe she wants more melodrama. Who knows?

Donnie sits on the grass, even though it's slightly moist, even though he can already imagine the brown stain seeping

into the fabric of his pants. He wishes he had a makeshift chair—
a rock or a stump or jutting root, something. No luck. Donnie
doesn't have anything to sit on in the car either, and even if he
did he'd have to go all the way down to the road and fetch it, one
more thing to remember. Donnie always makes sure he doesn't
leave anything up here. This is a sacred place, and it needs to be
treated with care. He won't have sex on the hill, or drink, or
make bonfires. It's not that sort of place. But this is the
downside of purifying the hill: wet pants. Oh well, he thinks. If
I'm going to be wet, I'll be wet. His mother will surely give him
hell, he thinks. Then let it come. Donnie leans back and lets his
body rest upon the grass. The sunshine is warm, and the breeze
is a gentle and unconditional caress. He. Slowly. Falls. Asleep.
In the back of his mind he can feel sweat drool down his neck
and the moisture leak into his clothes from below. But the
breeze. The breeze.

Then a faint metallic jingle.

"Donnie….Donnie….Hey.   Goofball…Look   at   this
spectacle. Donnie. Up and at 'em." Janet stands above him, a nest
of corkscrew curls obscuring the sunshine. She's wearing a black
silk dress, patterned with amorphous orange and yellow
explosions. Her wrists are encircled in ten or twelve bracelets
each—her arms resemble some 19th century industrial lever.
The jangle. The jingle. She buys bangles and bracelets on every
excursion.

Donnie blinks off his disorientation. He feels the
dampness on his back and legs and watches breeze stir the tree
fronds above. He glances over the houses and the stores and
blinks.

"When did you get here?" Donnie asks.

"Two. Right on the dot."

"What time is it?"

"Three minutes after two. Once again, you were dead to the world, you know." Janet bends down, inches from his face, twisting her head to get a closer look. Her eyes flicker over his skin, his clothes, over his body. "Where's your watch?"

"I don't know. I just realized that I don't—"

"Oh, boy."

"No, it's just that I don't really have it with me."

"Here we go."

"What? 'Here we go' what?"

"God, Donnie. When are you going to get with the program? It's 2001. We've been dating for…what? Sixteen or seventeen months."

"Don't you remem—it's year and a half next week."

"And you've lost three watches. You lose your keys all the time. You almost lost your wallet." She bends down and raps him on the head. "What's with you, seriously?" Janet snorts, and kicks at the grass in annoyance. Donnie closes his eyes. She's got it together. He doesn't. Same old story.

"I don't know." Donnie has a hard time standing up to Janet's jibes. She calls him "Pig-pen," and says he looks as if he just came from Woodstock. Donnie nods. Still, Janet rubs her hands on his head, and says she's proud of him for going through with the haircut. She kisses him, and grinds herself against him. She rubs his head, saying he looks sexy without hair. Donnie misses the times when they would cuddle each other in her parent's basement and listen to her father's old jazz records. He misses sharing Popsicles and wiping his sticky blue fingers on her neck. Now it's right to the issue. Sex. Something has been gained, but more has been lost. Not innocence exactly, but a kind of lighthearted play. He knows he shouldn't feel this way, but he does. His stomach knots.

"You look a lot less *mangy*," Janet says.

"I was mangy?"

"Sometimes it was a bit out of control. You were a yeti."

This is exactly the sort of micro-management that makes Donnie squirm. As much as he is annoyed by his mother's input into his daily life decisions, he seems to have found a parallel in Janet. He just wants to run away. If she wants to see other guys, that's her own problem. But don't tell me what to do or how to look, Donnie thinks. I never do that. This is exactly why he can't imagine living with her. His mother wants him to commit, and Janet thought it was a good idea. Forget it. Donnie has no desire to be around anybody for that amount of time. He pulls away from her. He doesn't want to spoil this place.

Janet scowls at him. Donnie hates that glower—more than anything.

"So what did you want to talk about?" Donnie has carried around a rock in his gut all day. He'd rather confront it now, free himself up. Janet takes his hands and swings them in hers. One of the bracelets snags his left wrist.

"Donnie," she says. "I've been thinking."

Donnie releases one of his hands in preparation. By her suddenly coiled posture and tone Donnie can tell this isn't going to be good news. As he suspected.

"I can't come to the beach with you all. I mean, I want to. I just—"

"What? Are you kidding me? We've been—"

"I'm *not* coming with you, Donnie. I'm sorry."

Donnie realizes he should have expected this. She is unreliable, and yet wants *him* to grow up. She's the only reason he was interested in the prospect of an ocean vacation. Without her, forget it. He doesn't want a family vacation. He doesn't want forced togetherness. His parents will grate on his last nerve in about three hours, and he'll be absolutely miserable. There's Kevin, but that's not enough.

"You have to go. You are why *I'm* going. That's the only reason I agreed to go. You have to go. That was the whole— we've been planning this for weeks, for months."

"I don't *have* to do anything," she says, releasing his other hand.

"Fine," Donnie says. "Okay."

"Honestly, I just don't feel like it…really," she says.

"Well…Jesus. You're not supposed to meet us until—"

"I know. But it's not happening. I just don't *feel* like it. That's the thing. I just don't feel it."

Donnie shakes his head and turns towards the woods, and sets foot on the path away from Janet. He thinks about telling her how she always disappoints him, how she always lets him down at key moments, how he can't depend on her. But he knows she'll use her cold-fish rant, her statement against the sort of milquetoast guy he has become. His lack of ambition. His lack of willpower. Donnie walks down the path toward the road. The wind is in his ears, and he can smell the trees and bushes and the weeds underneath.

"Donnie," Janet says behind him. "Don't be an asshole. That's the number one rule."

The wind is in his ears, and he can smell the spruce trees all around him. He knows it's over.

The tree shadows chop through the drive home. Sun, shadow, sun, shadow. Donnie tries to avoid thinking. Then he tries to avoid thinking about avoiding thinking. Down the hilly road towards home he's stuck behind a dump truck. Sand and dirt clods ping his windshield, and the truck's apron thrashes like a livid appendage. Donnie flips to the classical station, and listens to Brahms. He recognizes the symphony from his music history class. Forgets the name. He could never keep those things straight. He should be irritated about the dump truck. But he's not. He's in no hurry to get on with the rest of the day.

Parking the car in the driveway, Donnie steps into the cool interior of his parents' house. He has spent the last eleven years of his life here and he can only remember the blurry outlines of his early childhood in Baltimore. Everything seemed so vertical then: a slender townhouse in the city, more of the same around him, buildings in the immediate distance. The horizon was stunted until they hit the highway. Now the general pattern is horizontal and diagonal for the most part, and he has to seek out what he once knew. He misses it. There is something unfussy and pragmatic about the city that is lacking in the burbs. The limitation the city imposes establishes a kind of freedom, Donnie thinks. Geography isn't everything, but it's something.

"Oh, you're home. Good." His mother stands from her litter of paperwork towering on her small corner desk, and she flops a couple of grilled cheese sandwiches on the stove. Donnie sits at the kitchen table and opens the morning paper. He didn't even look at it over breakfast, but then breakfast was a bagel and apple juice at noon.

"Look at you. I can actually see your *face*." His mother beams. Donnie thinks: there's nothing she likes more than a well-groomed man. That's probably how she ended up with dad—probably the only guy in 1971 that brushed his hair and wore a bow tie. "Did it take long?"

"No, no. Not too long." Donnie eyes the clock—three thirty. "What time are we leaving?"

"In about an hour. Are you all packed?" This is a central difference between Donnie and his mother. She prepares, plans-ahead, sees the future as a direct continuum of the past. Donnie is impulsive, idiosyncratic. He doesn't want to change for his mother, for Janet, for anybody. He is who he is who he is.

Donnie can predict the barrage of complaints that will rain upon him if he says no. This is what his life had come to. He's a full-grown adult, and yet at every moment of his waking life he feels crimped. Claustrophobia sets in. He can't wait to move out, but he can't afford it; he has little motivation or means. At times the end result is complete frustration.

Sometimes Donnie just throws his hands up and lets his mother say whatever she wants without reproach. This is his method with Janet as well. It must please them to hear acquiescence, he thinks. It must make them feel some sense of direction over chaos. But I *am* chaos, he thinks. If I weren't, would I be in this position? Then immediately he feels utterly pretentious.

"Just about," he says.

"Good. Don't forget a sweater and some jeans. You remember how cold it gets at night."

"Okay."

"Is Janet excited?"

"Oh yes. Yeah. Very much so."

His mother slides the grilled cheese onto a plate for him, sloughs a pile of chips next to the sandwiches, and hands Donnie a glass of water. The squares of bread ooze orange lava. The center of the square is charred, but the crust isn't. Donnie pokes his finger into the cheese and lifts it to his mouth. He's trying to smell whether it's mild or sharp cheese, but he can't tell. He wipes his finger on his plate. His mother is usually a great cook, even with grilled cheese.

"There's fruit on the table," she points.

"So what are you doing right now?"

"I'm getting ready for the trip." She sits next to him and pats his head and nods.

"No, I mean with the paperwork you have there?"

"Bills. You know how it is."

"Not really," Donnie says, biting into the first of his sandwiches. His fall class schedule rattles in his mind: Economics, Business, Science Fiction 2, Social Problems and History of Science. Perhaps his mother is right. Perhaps he should get a job. He could cut back three credits. Maybe six. It would take him longer, but it might be worth the trade-off. He'd think on it. The only thing: what to do?

"Where's Dad?"

"Where do you think?" She points upstairs. The den. The lair. Sometimes Donnie feels his father's up to no good. Just a feeling. In a dream he had last week his father was a wasp. He hid in the curtains, waiting for Donnie to pass by. That was it. Just an image. These image-dreams happen all the time.

"Have any idea, by the way, where my watch might be?"

"Uh, nope. Sorry, Charlie," his mother replies. She's in a

good mood, maybe because she can feel a sense of accomplishment; he's a *project* heading in the right direction.

Donnie finishes his lunch and drops his plate in the dishwasher. This is when his mother notices the brown smudges on his pants and shirt. She asks him how that got there and Donnie shrugs. He says he was spread-eagled on the grass watching the clouds roll by—more or less the truth—that he didn't notice that the grass was wet until it was too late. Donnie gives it the tone of a minor tragedy. His mother shakes her head.

"A dreamer until the end," she says. Donnie smiles and walks down the hall.

Upstairs Donnie folds shorts, T-shirts, his swimming trunks, and towels into a duffel bag. He remembers his jeans and a sweater for the chillier evenings. He tosses deodorant, razors, a toothbrush and toothpaste in a plastic bag, and crams that in the duffel bag. He brings along *The Gay Science* and *Beyond Good and Evil* more for confidence and moral ballast than reading material. He hasn't read Nietzsche in two years and he's not sure he can again, really. But he likes having Friedrich along for protection. He packs condoms. You never know, Donnie thinks. He thinks about bringing his pillow, but this seems too infantile somehow. Too Charlie Brown.

As he's searching aimlessly for his watch, Kevin's frizz of blonde hair puffs around the doorframe.

"Hey bro," he says. "What's cooking?"

Donnie shrugs.

"Are you ready for the fun-fest or what?"

Donnie nods. He wonders if he should bring some music along. But nobody listens to classical music. Wait a minute, he thinks.

"Wait a minute," he says.

"What? What's going on?"

He opens his duffel bag and removes the shorts and T-shirts. He opens his closet and snaps slacks and dress shirts from their hangers.

"What are you doing?"

"Everyone always wears shorts and T-shirts at the beach. Why not something else? I'm going in *style*." Donnie starts folding slacks and dress shirts into the duffel bag. He finds his nice shoes and black socks, undershirts and cuff links. He tucks them all into the duffel bag, smiling. This is the first time he's felt free all day. She wants me to be well dressed; I'll be debonair when I'm not supposed to be.

"You're letting her get to you too much. Just relax." This is Kevin's typical stance on life, Donnie thinks. He is more apt to hits the brakes than the gas. He is a good balance for me, Donnie thinks.

"Maybe," Donnie says. "It'll be an experiment."

"Okay then. Well, you're riding with mom then. Have a blast."

"We're taking two cars?"

"Yeah."

"Oh," Donnie says. He feels deflated. Oh well.

Donnie remembers they would always take one car on family trips. The two kids in the backseat, and their parents in the front seat. It's wasn't always the picture of family bliss—kids singing songs and playing I Spy—but they were all *together*. There was a sense of unity that Donnie is nostalgic about suddenly. This surprises him. Then five years ago they suddenly took two cars on their family vacations—North Carolina, Florida, White Mountains and Chicago. Everything was separate.

His parents say it's because they have too much stuff, but they could always get one of those baggage carriers that fit on top of your car. If he pressed them, Donnie knows their logic would completely collapse. This is no good, Donnie thinks, and it doesn't bode well. But Kevin smiles, seems willing to go with the flow. This makes it easier, his smile seems to say. No worries.

After packing one car with clothes, books, food, beach toys, blankets, and towels Donnie sits in the front seat while his mother walks around the house checking the windows and doors, making sure the instructions for the cat are clear for the sitter. She goes over everything ten times, Donnie thinks. When will she let go? His father sits in the other car, sunglasses on, the engine running and the air-conditioning on full-blast. His head is in his hands. He looks wretched. Kevin sits in the passenger seat, rocking back and forth. His father's head snaps at Kevin and he says something. Kevin nods. Winces.

Donnie watches the heat rise from his father's car. The grass is brown near the driveway, and the flowers are drying from lack of rain. Then his mother closes the front door, and turns to lock it, and walks to the car. Her face looks firm, and she slips her sunglasses on, and for some reason the glasses remind Donnie of a veil.

"Let's go," she says, snapping the driver's side door closed. "We have a long drive ahead of us." Donnie's mother glances over at her husband. He stares back. For a second

Donnie sees Kevin and his father as a sort of mirror, and he feels sorry for his father. Donnie can imagine himself in a similar spot in life. God help me, Donnie thinks. The trick, Donnie thinks, is to not put himself in that position. That's the key. Then his mother briskly pulls the car down the driveway. They drive down Cedar Lane.

"So talk to Mommy then," Donnie's mother is saying in a mock-cutesy voice. They are scuttling down Route 50, weaving in front of tractor-trailers, passing pickup trucks on the right hand side. This is his mother's favorite catch phrase, but Donnie doesn't feel like talking. He's content to listen to the Mozart concerto fade in and out on the local radio station. He likes watching cornfields glaze by. He likes that for miles and miles he will see nothing but fields, only broken by the occasional gas station or Kentucky Fried Chicken in the middle of nowhere. Then it's back to cornfields. He likes the airing out—stretching his vision.

"I mean, if you think that he's ignoring you, let's talk about it. Let's hash it out, and then we can bring our discoveries to him *that* way."

Then Donnie makes the mistake of mentioning that his father seems to spend more and more time in the den recently. He rarely verbalizes these observations. Be a Stoic, or at least make a pass at it. He only says this to fill the empty space, and then he immediately regrets it. Donnie knows how much his mother wants to talk, analyze and parse the truth of a statement. He should know better.

But his mother doesn't miss her opportunity to jump on it. She draws out more observations from her Socratic grilling.

She wants to find the truth of the matter, as if the fate of the world rests upon it. Somehow she is even able to get Donnie to imply a certain level of resentment or distrust. He feels these emotions, but he doesn't want to admit to them. But she has a way of extracting a confession. She's a magician, Donnie thinks, there's no way around it.

"Mom," he says. "I don't want to create....I'm just—"

"The only problem will be if you *don't* say anything. If you don't say anything then what you are implying is that your life isn't worth improving. Is that the kind of life you want to live? No. I'm telling you it's not."

"Okay. Okay."

Donnie stares out the window again. He can't stand the artificial Freon smell of the air-conditioning. He'd prefer to switch the A.C. off and just open the car windows, but his mother would say the humidity is frizzing her hair, frying her mind.

"Look, do me a favor," she says.

"What's that?"

"In the cooler in the back seat there are some Dove bars. Why don't you and I sneak a couple of them? I mean, Jesus, let's spoil ourselves for once, huh? Whadda ya say?"

"Okay." Donnie roots under the blankets and towels and opens the lid to the cooler. Inside there is fruit, cold cuts, cheese, sodas, and in the corner of the cooler, Dove bars. Donnie opens the package and pulls out two bars. He unwraps one and hands it to his mother. He unwraps the other and takes a bite.

"Now," his mother says. "Let's try again."

Donnie thinks about his mother's behavior and predictable attitude. Since she works as a guidance counselor at a local middle school, her thinking is engrained in verbal affirmation. Since her own mother raised her to cook and eat well, she orients her happiness around ice cream and fried squash and penne and chicken noodle soup made from scratch. Since she likes to blow off steam, she goes on spending orgies. Donnie supposes he is just as predictable, but he hopes he's not *that* predictable. It's just a matter of muddying routines, he thinks. She doesn't smoke now that he knows of, but she used to. He wonders if she still craves cigarettes.

"Let's talk about it later, okay?"

His mother nods in agreement, downing the rest of the ice cream bar. He gnaws his bar to a stub.

"That's fine. We'll have plenty of time to talk on this trip," she says. "Plenty of time."

Donnie nods. He only defers the difficulties, nothing more. He watches the cornfields slide by and ravens plunge into them and rise back up into the distant line of trees.

At Route 13 they take back roads to the beach, the flat Eastern Shore roads that bypass Ocean City to the North. Donnie's eyes flicker to follow the billboards and clapboard houses. Everything seems faded by the sun, or perhaps it's the fact that the sun bleaches what he sees as he sees it. Or perhaps there is some subtle optical illusion that tricks his mind into thinking that physically everything seems whitewashed because so much seems psychologically faded. Donnie wonders which one of these is the truth. His mother would know.

He also wonders how long it will take his mother to realize that Janet is not meeting them after all. Once she does find out, he has no idea how she will react. He's not even sure his mother likes Janet. They might be too similar, though his mother definitely is softer around the edges. One thing is for sure: he doesn't want pity.

Donnie imagines Janet on the phone, calling guys she met here and there. She probably feels liberated. With the cat away, she can take her desires and run with them. Whatever becomes of this, Donnie thinks, it can't be positive. The snowball is in full motion. It's just a matter of time.

Donnie watches corrugated aluminum produce stands whiz by every mile or so on this stretch of road. Donnie's mother wants to stop at one to buy corn, and tomatoes, and cucumbers, and zucchini. She blinks her lights at her husband's car in front of them, but he doesn't pull over.

"Damnit, Gary," she says, as if her husband is in the car with her. "Pull over." She flicks her lights faster. "I told you I wanted to stop for vegetables. You're the one who likes corn on the cob. I don't even like it." She beeps her horn, and then presses her elbow into it.

Donnie presses his forehead to the passenger side window. Ugh. A butterfly is caught in the windshield wipers. It pivots, trying to free itself, and then the wind flings it free. One white wing is still pinned under the right wiper. It flutters in the wind, snags on the edge of the hood. Then the wind blows that off as well.

Finally Donnie's father pulls over onto the grass shoulder to the right of the produce stand. They both pull into the gravel parking lot, fuming clouds into the dry grass surrounding the produce stand. Donnie watches his father prop his chin in his hands. Kevin nods to his Walkman. Their mouths don't move. His mother slams the car door and tears a plastic bag from a nail on one of the posts holding the flimsy structure upright. She walks over to the corn.

When she's done Donnie's mother piles the bags of produce at Donnie's feet. "There's no room in the trunk," she says. "Just be careful not to step on the tomatoes." Donnie slides his feet under the base of the dashboard, feeling the air-conditioning chill his feet. At least something is cool around here, he thinks. Donnie's father peels back onto the road in front of them. Kevin's head bobs.

After cruising down the short stretch of lights and strip malls, they pull into the parking lot for the condominium community, a massive series of eleven towers lining the beach. Donnie watches his father step out of his car and walk into the office. Kevin pops the passenger door and stretches. Donnie wants to walk around. Behind him is the highway, to the right one of the many outdoor pools, and to the left a stripe of bushes dividing the condo parking lot from the adjacent strip of stores and restaurants. Donnie follows his father into the office.

A wave of air-conditioning smacks Donnie in the face as he opens the door to the office, and an electronic doorbell clangs to the tune of "Twinkle Twinkle Little Star." His father stands third in line inside the roped-off faux-corridor, arms crossed. A woman with muscled shoulders and spiked auburn hair is telling a couple about the amenities—hot tubs, pools, gyms, game rooms. You could stay here all week and never set foot on the beach, Donnie thinks. His father stares at him, looking him over.

"So, they have lots of things to do here, it seems."

"Yeah," Donnie says.

"It should be relaxing," his father says. "We can all do

whatever we want. No agenda." His back is stiff. He doesn't look relaxed.

"It should be," Donnie says.

On the speakers they are playing a dinky-dink-dink-dink xylophone cover of "Sweet Heart of Mine" by Guns and Roses.

"How did you find out about this place anyway?" Other than relying on frail pleasantries, Donnie feels as if he should initiate something approaching conversation.

"A good friend of mine," he says. "From the congregation. She said it was very pleasant."

"That's nice," Donnie says. "Who is that?"

"Just a member from the congregation."

"Anyone I know?"

"No, she's a new member. A very nice lady. A good friend."

"Oh."

The rug pattern is pale green squares with pink borders separating each square. The office walls are papered in small blue flowers with yellow fringes. So far everything about this place strikes Donnie as having an inside and an outside. You are part of us, or you are on the outside of us. He wasn't surprised to hear the representative tell them they had to carry their badge around with them at all times so the lifeguards would be able to identify them as "members," rather than predatory intruders bent on raping and pillaging.

"Each badge will cost you twenty five dollars," she says. For a moment her fake eyelashes gnash together like a Venus flytrap. Gary hands the woman a credit card, and she hands him the keys. How easy it is to turn plastic to metal, Donnie thinks.

Donnie follows his father back out into the parking lot.

The bits of broken glass on the highway glint in the sun. The parking lot is pristine asphalt, freshly tarred.

As they walk back to their respective cars, his father taps Donnie's shoulder. Odd, Donnie thinks. I'm right here.

"Do me a favor," his father says.

"What's that?" Donnie says.

"Try to get your mother to *settle down* before we get inside. You know, if you can. I know it's a difficult task with her. She's a bit out of control. Give it a shot though, bucko."

Donnie stares blankly, then nods slightly. He doesn't like this one bit.

"That-a-boy," his father says.

Donnie has a vivid sense of déjà vu suddenly. They are circling for the two reserved parking spaces in the condominium lots that curl under the building in an open-air garage and sprawl out towards the highway. The spaces are numbered and lettered, but they aren't in order. Donnie's father is losing his temper at the system (or lack thereof), and his mother is wringing her hands, peering nervously around each column under the building. Donnie steps out of the car and decides to look on foot. Kevin does the same.

Donnie and Kevin sweep the parking lots for 32A and 45B, with little luck. Kevin takes the garage portion, and Donnie is out in the sun. His parents slowly circle the parking lot in their respective cars. Most of the spots are filled with station wagons and mini-vans and SUVs. For a moment if feels as if the whole family is wandering through a craggy desert landscape searching for each other. At one point Donnie can't see his parents or Kevin. It's as if he's a boy again, lost in Safeway.

Mommy where are you?

Donnie asks the security guard in the booth, but he just tells Donnie to look at the map in the condominium lobby. The sun beats against the black asphalt and radiates upward in waves of heat. The bushes and cars obscure his vision. He feels misplaced and confused and wanders for what seems to be hours. The heat curdles his brain.

Then he hears Kevin call out. "I've got 45B," he shouts. Donnie runs toward the sound. He can't remember the last time he was so relieved. When he crosses under the building into the shade Donnie sees Kevin waving his arms back and forth, then his mother cruising toward the spot from the right. Smiling and waving. Kevin shuffles off to the side as Donnie approaches. The brothers slap hands.

"Way to go," Donnie says. "I was dying out there."

"Hey, no biggie."

Donnie's mother steps out of the car, stretching. She tells them that their father said he is parking in the auxiliary lot past the entrance. Gave up.

"Go and help your father, Donnie."

Donnie walks out of the shade, back into the glare. His father briskly walks past carrying his suitcase and a bag of towels.

"The trunk is unlocked," he says, pointing to where the car rests.

Donnie opens the trunk and grabs a suitcase, a bag of food, and slides the lime green beach umbrella under his arm. As he carries them towards the garage and the stairs under the cool shade of it, Donnie imagines each item as a representation of the family unit, as if each bears a family secret or nugget of pain or pleasure yet uttered. This part is my burden, he thinks. We all carry our weight, and this is mine.

As he walks up the stairs gritted with sand, Donnie hums Mozart. It stuck. Then he walks down the outside corridor and knocks on the condo door. Kevin opens the door briskly and laughs.

"What took you so long?"

"I had to walk through the damn desert," Donnie says.

Kevin shakes his head, and Donnie waves it off. Donnie props the umbrella in the corner and places the bag and suitcase on the table in the front room. His parents stand on the balcony overlooking the evening ocean and the slant of sun hitting the froth and the birds darting in and out of it. His mother is off to the right, clear of the sliding glass door and her hair curls in the wind. His father stands in the doorway, as if he doesn't want to commit to the waves.

For a moment nobody speaks, and they listen to the thrum of the waves. Gorgeous. This is the pinnacle, Donnie thinks. The ocean is all downhill from here. It's that first kiss, that moment of almost painful anticipation fulfilled. From this point on, we'll take it for granted. It will be there, but it will have a watered down hazy feel to it. Donnie's parents continue to watch.

Kevin cuffs Donnie on the shoulder.

"Let's take a look around," Kevin says.

They walk to the right, through a narrow hallway carpeted in an aqua blue shag—the color people wish the ocean actually was. The room to the right is small, decorated with a white wicker bed, seashell pastels, and wallpaper with a pattern of seagulls, buoys, and sunglasses in a triangular pattern. Great, Donnie thinks. Just once I'd like to see a condo that doesn't reference seashells or the breeze or the sun.

"That's your room," Donnie says.

"No way," Kevin says. "You get the girl's room."

"Let's see this one first," Donnie says.

They push the door open to find a larger space with two single beds, and an underwater theme. The walls are a dark blue, and the lamps are decorated with faux-fishnets and seaweed. A shelf on the far wall holds starfish shells, conch shells, and cracked bones of driftwood. The beds are angled to look like rowboats equipped with fake oars at the base.

Donnie and Kevin loop back through the dining room, into the kitchen decked-out in pinkish hued cabinets. The living room is decorated with more wicker and throw pillows adorned in tropical fish prints, and rubber plants guarding either side of the couches. The master bedroom bears a jungle theme with a leopard print bed and an overhead fan made of faux palm fronds.

Even from this enclave they can hear the waves. When they return to the deck their parents stand in the same position, staring out over the beach, the sun only skimming the deck to the pool, the beach, the froth and slow waves lapping in from the west. Below three men in baseball caps wave their metal detectors back and forth over the sand. A family flies a kite that looks like an oversized bolo tie. Seagulls squawk unseen overhead.

After dinner that night, Kevin and Donnie unpack their bags, and watch television and play cards and their parents continue to unpack. They recline on the wicker couches, listening to the wind rattle the windows. Donnie watches his mother glower and his dad read a book. Donnie watches his father ignoring her. She pretends not to care.

Kevin goes to bed, and after half an hour his parents shuffle to their room, and click the door closed. Donnie sits in the darkness, the lights from the pool area leaking up through the balcony, forming a pale trapezoid on the rug.

Donnie thinks of his hair clippings stuffed in a plastic bag behind Carl's store with the dust-covered hair of others. Part of him mixed with parts of many others. Strange, he thinks. He pats his shorn head, but that makes him feel worse.

Donnie feels a looming sense of dread and doom. Something ominous is on the horizon. He can feel it in his gut, a smoldering. The wind gusts rush harder, and Donnie can hear sand ping against the deck at the base of the condo. He can hear his parents talking in their room, their voices rising. He can hear his father. "That's *not* true, Janice. Why are you always dragging your heals?" For a moment Donnie imagines the whole sandy beach turned to glass. Then what?

"Gary, that's not fair. At all. And it's just not the way it is," his mother says. "You know that as well as I do."

His own goal over this week is to stop thinking. Donnie wants to calm the impulse to analyze and justify, to pick apart. Focusing on the world around him would be nice. Making the world in his head disappear would be even nicer. We'll start with a relaxing sleep, Donnie thinks. A good one. I want a good sleep that will link into other good sleeps down the road. That will be a start. Then what?

Donnie looks out over the balcony in the darkness. The glass rattles in the wind, and he feels a knot in his stomach. He closes his eyes, but images flood him: the image of the butterfly wing in the windshield wiper; spruce trees lining the path to the hill; Carl's mole; his mother eating a surreptitious Dove bar.

He decides to practice something his friend Victor taught him. He breathes deeply then he exhales the poisoned thoughts from him. He does this four times, and for a moment the wind abates for a moment. Inhale. Exhale. Inhale. Exhale. In. Out. In. Out.

As Donnie walks down the hallway to the bedroom, he can hear the wind pick up again. Darkness overcomes him and he feels his way through it.

Saturday

In the back recesses of his mind Donnie hears noises. Clinking. Bubbling. Muffled bursts of laughter. He rolls over, and pulls the comforter over his head. The light is still limp and washed-out, and Donnie thinks it must be eight in the morning, perhaps eight thirty. Far too early for a vacation. He falls back asleep, dreaming of flying in a cargo airplane packed with animals.

Later, when Donnie wakes up, the condo is silent and the sun shoots through the curtains. He clicks his mouth, tugs at his ear, and rolls his neck. The condo pillow is too big and the back of his neck is stiff. He knew he should have brought his favorite pillow. Donnie sits up in bed and wonders what he will do with his time. This is what prisoners must contend with all the time.

Donnie shuffles to the outside world. A note sits under a green saucer on the dining room table on piece of yellow-lined legal paper with a key next to it: "Donnie—went to beach. We're off to the right from the pool. Come join us when you get up. Mom." He crunches the paper into a ball, spins it on the table top and peeks on the kitchen counter to survey the breakfast offerings. A bowl of fruit—bananas, apples, oranges, kiwi—sits next to the coffee maker. Boxes of cereal sit on top of the refrigerator, and Donnie pours himself a bowl, and heats up a mug of coffee for himself. He looks at the clock on the stove—10:14.

What is Donnie to do here, anyway? He knows he should call Janet today. That's for sure. But then what? Then what? He can hear the waves. In the kiddy pool a baby yelps.

As Donnie spoons his cereal, he takes a look around him. On the wall perpendicular to the kitchen are two garish paintings—one of a hummingbird, and one of a manatee. Both paintings are on the frame glass itself. By the front door is a pot of reeds, and a woven hanging marked with two Xs divided by a vertical line, and topped with a large black diamond shape. Black tassels hang from the weaving, almost down to the rug. In the morning light the chandelier looks like a pulsating Portuguese Man-o-war. This condo *is* something else, he thinks. Unusual, worthy of some sort of scrutiny.

Donnie dreads the thought of talking to Janet, and especially of becoming the focus of his mother's attention and concern. If he can do it without any parental notice, all the better. He doesn't like the idea of holding secrets, but he does want to enjoy his vacation. This is top priority number one.

Donnie plops his mug and bowl in the dishwasher and breathes deeply, then exhales. Breathes deeply, then exhales. Breathes deeply, then exhales.

Shower and shave. Donnie dresses in his Sunday best. The time is right. It's the sort of suit he used to see his grandfather wear to funerals: a glossy navy blue cotton and polyester blend with gold buttons. Everything shiny. The buttons remind Donnie of a sailor's. He wears his patent leather shoes. He polishes them with a paper towel, and peers at his own muddled reflection in the glow. His face is muted and pallid. He positions his reflection in the middle of his laces. He grins and laces up through the image of his own face. This will be something, he thinks.

Donnie clicks the outside door closed and bounds down the stairwell down to the parking garage, and takes a sharp left to the wooden pool deck. Then he walks by. He watches the glances, the glares, the question marks. He knows it's a childish game, but what the Hell. His father. His mother. His brother. Somehow he fits into this family lattice. He wants another cup of coffee and a newspaper. He wants to embrace the self-important and exclusive. Role-playing for my own amusement, Donnie thinks. It doesn't get any more pathetic. We cope in our own ways.

As Donnie walks along the edge of the water in the lemony light the children drop their shovels and beach balls. Mothers turn to their husbands. Young girls shake their heads. Guys laugh outright. The waves lap the soles of his dress shoes, and sand kicks up under his pants cuffs, and around his socks. This feels good, Donnie thinks. This is going to be an excellent trip. There is unlimited opportunity here. Friends can be made. Sex can be had. Moles can be scrutinized. Then there is the beach, the unlimited sky and sun. It feels healthy and liberating. At the beach nobody trusts a man in a suit.

Donnie thinks about past family vacations. Each one had

a similar arc. The trip to Denver two years ago was so promising at the outset, with seemingly unlimited entertainment on the horizon. By mid-week the family had fragmented into separate activities, each member pursuing their own interests: Kevin went to a baseball game, Mom on a culinary tour, Dad hid inside and read, and Donnie walked the streets. Family trips always begin with such sunny optimism, but end with clouds and the eventual signs of family implosion.

No. This one will be different, Donnie thinks. With Janet he would find himself stuck in boyfriend mode all the time. I'd have to entertain her. She'd tell me what to wear, what to think, what to say. Without Janet, the prospects open up, Donnie rationalizes. I can walk down the beach in a suit if I want. I can walk down the beach naked if I want. At least for a few minutes.

He can hear the murmurings. Some guy blurts out, "Hey buddy, whadda ya forget to look in the mirror this morning?" Why does he care? Donnie doesn't get it. Donnie watches the froth claw at the sand. The wind whips at the fabric, pastes it to his body. The sun radiates off the dark suit, and Donnie feels a dollop of sweat trickle down his back. This is fine, he thinks. Let it come.

Donnie was known in high school as a starer, an oddball who didn't have the politeness to look away. Girls told him he made them feel uncomfortable. Teachers thought he was strange. His friends would tell him it's not such a good idea to gape unless he wants a fight. "It's just a matter of time," they'd say. "Some guy is going to think…and then…" This idea just made Donnie want to stare even more. If Donnie was attracted to a girl he'd gawp all the livelong day. He knows this. He'd stare a hole right through her head.

In fact, Donnie can't remember a time when he *didn't* like to look. He was just curious at first, and then in second grade he realized staring is one way to make Jimmy Falkner edgy. At lunch he'd eyeball Jimmy without blinking until Jimmy either told him to stop or left the table. He realized that this made people squirm—that he could wield it as a kind of weapon. He didn't care how they responded; he wanted to provoke a charge out of them, forcing them to notice his presence. But more: Donnie wanted to feel as if he had some *sway*.

In his suit and tie ensemble, Donnie walks into the beach shop littered with sand pails, suntan lotion, T-shirts, flip flops, towels, salt-water taffy, and Frisbees. On the store's right side an aisle is devoted to shells. Seated in the middle of the third aisle is a woman bent over a pile of plastic shovels with hair as knotted and tangled as the seaweed washed up with the daily flotsam and jetsam. As he looks closer Donnie notices her hair contains *actual* seaweed. Her back is to Donnie and she shoots price stickers onto the business end of each orange and yellow shovel. Donnie stands in the doorway staring. This is where I am supposed to be, he thinks. At this moment this is what I am supposed to be doing.

Slowly Donnie walks along the first aisle of the store where aspirin and toothpaste fill bins in casual mounds. Mini-deodorants. Mouthwash. He peeks at the seaweed woman through the shelving units. Another woman—stubby and sun burnt—steps out of the back and approaches Donnie.

"Can I help you with something?" Her eyes look forlorn and half-asleep. Tinge of frustration in her tight mouth.

But Donnie watches the back of the woman on the floor.

He tells himself he hopes that she won't turn around. If she stays exactly where she is, Donnie knows that he could have a goldmine to discover later. There is something about her, he thinks. She is an ambiguity in search of some sort of clarification. As it is, Donnie knows nothing about her. But Donnie goes on gut feeling, and his gut feeling is telling him she could be won over. But she can't turn around. *Don't turn around.* Then he surges from the store before she notices him.

At the newspaper box Donnie stops and slips two quarters in. He rolls the newspaper under his arm and buys a cup of bitter coffee from the funnel cake stand, sipping it as he walks back down the beach toward his family. He doesn't look back. He bites on the Styrofoam.

Donnie plops himself down on the green beach blanket next to his mother. She's spread on her stomach, flipping through an issue of *Newsweek* with little concern for the articles. She lingers on the ads, lingers on the pages with photographs. She has a towel over her head even though she's sprawled in the shade of the umbrella.

"Hi there, kiddo," she says without looking up.

"Hey."

"Oh, I forgot to leave a note."

"What?"

"Janet called this morning," she says.

"She did?"

"The phone's in the beach bag." She looks up at Donnie, noticing his attire. Shakes her head. Donnie figures she thinks he's vying for attention, trying too hard, and maybe this is the sum of what he's after. But aside from the shake, she doesn't respond. A more elaborate response would help, but instead she flips the page of the magazine. Donnie sighs. He wishes he could afford a car phone. His friends are all getting them. Texting. Talk about freedom! Or the even better—a more expensive cell phone, something like the one his mother has.

"I thought it was going to rain today," she says. "I mean the wind last night was really strong."

"Yeah, but it's sunny. It always seems to be sunny at the beach," Donnie says.

"What a sense of optimism," she says. "How wonderful." She pats his knee.

"Where's Kev?"

"He met some friends already. Isn't that something? A group of kids needed another volleyball player, apparently, and they asked Kevin." This is the difference between Kevin and me, Donnie thinks. Kevin's a volleyball glad-hander. I'm not.

Donnie nods and peers down the strand towards the volleyball net. Donnie can only see a blur of people in bathing suits. It's too far to tell if Kevin is there or not.

"Go call Janet before she's gone. It's Sunday after all. Isn't she coming out today?"

"Yeah, I'll call her," Donnie says. He roots around in the beach bag until he finds the black rectangle of plastic. He stands up and walks toward the water, opening the phone.

"Hey, Donnie," his mother calls after him. "Don't make it a long call. Low on batteries."

Donnie nods and then snaps the phone closed again. He sits on a shelf of sand by the water. His stomach balls up and he feels queasy. He tries the breathing again, but it doesn't take. He closes his eyes and listens to the sounds of the waves.

As he listens to the digital rings, Donnie thinks about how this particular phone call just fits into a larger, unpleasant pattern. The beach seems to leave a bad taste in his mouth. This is not new. When he was thirteen he was a member of a teen tour— amusement parks, hikes, the city, the beach. He met a girl with braids and freckles. Cute, elfin, a bit younger. Donnie fell immediately in love with her, though he barely knew her. By the time they made it to the Ocean City boardwalk, she let him down hard. He spent the entire trip wandering the boardwalk alone gumming dry cotton candy. Now he's in his twenties and still unable to escape the melodrama of the beach. And worse— he has to do it long-distance as a result of Janet's absence.

Four rings and Donnie hears laughter and slowly Janet's "hello." Her voice sounds airy and distant, as if she's outside. And sleepy.

"Where are you?"

"I decided to just take my own vacation right here," she says. "Just because you ran away doesn't mean I'm going to cry in my milk. No, sir."

"'Ran away'? Cut the shit, Janet."

"I'm at the poooo-oooooool," she says. Donnie can't stand her tendency towards petty one-upmanship. Janet lugs her own bags of rancor wherever she goes. I'm better off without her, Donnie thinks.

"I'm at the beeee-aaaach," Donnie says. "Jealous much?"

A breath. "So what made you take off with your tail between your legs?"

"What are you talking about?"

"The hill. Running away from your problems. Sound

familiar?"

The knot in Donnie's stomach is coagulating. This is exactly what he didn't want—more hard-edged ballbusting first thing in the morning. He closes his eyes and concentrates on the background surf, the sounds of kids playing in the sand around him, the smell of cocoa butter. Then on her end, he hears kids playing and splashing, and the moment is muddied.

"You're the one who—"

"Don't be so delicate," she says. "I'm joking." No she's not.

"Look—"

"You're just like your father, you know that? You say you're disgusted by the way he insulates himself to escape problems. Well? Blah, blah, blah, blah. Look in the mirror."

"Are you still joking?" Nothing. "The difference, Janet, is that I'm...you pushed *me* away. I wanted you to come. I'm not trying to escape my problems. I just want to be on vacation."

"Same here," Janet says. "Only not with you and the kin. I mean, honestly, Donnie. Can you imagine me making small talk with your *mother*? I mean...What, over cherry tomatoes? What would we talk about?"

"I'm not Nostradamus. How am I supposed to know how the two of you would get along?"

"No, you're something else altogether. But look at the past. Look at how it went then. Life is too short. Donnie, go ahead and do what you set out to do. I know that's why you called." He can imagine young muscled men smearing coconut oil into her naked backside right at this moment. He can imagine other less principled options readily appearing before her. This is what *she* wants, Donnie thinks. Fine. She has a long way to go towards anything approaching full-fledged adulthood.

"Why don't *you* end it?" Donnie says. At this he expects a back and forth. Janet will surely counter-offer, make concessions, deal with him as a three-dimensional human being filled with kindness and generosity.

"That's not a problem for me," she says. And the next sound Donnie hears is the dial tone. Like a smack. Donnie stumbles in the sand.

Donnie lurches back to the blanket, hands the phone back to his mother, and walks back to the condo in a daze. He can hear his mother calling after him, but he doesn't answer. It's not her business, he keeps telling himself. It's *his* affair, and he has to tend to it. It's not her business. The stairwell and corridors are a blur. Donnie feels limp.

He jiggles the lock open, but before he can turn the knob it opens from the inside. His father smiles at him, looking like a sedated version of the person he saw yesterday. He tries to ask Donnie what he's doing today, what he has planned, but Donnie breezes by without a word. He wants a shower.

"Hey," his father says. "Why are you all dressed up? Wedding today?"

"Hahahahaa."

Donnie opens the door to the bathroom and slips off his clothes off into a heap by the door. He turns on the water and waits for it to warm. He steps into the shower, allows the water to hammer his back and shoulders. The pounding jets of water. For a while Donnie doesn't move towards soap or shampoo. He thinks about sitting in the tub like a rape victim in a television melodrama. Forget it. Damn the Hollywood clichés. He does just that—sits in the tub, lets the water hit him from above.

I'm always watched, Donnie thinks. God is a camera. Imperceptibly the roll spools forever.

When Donnie shuts the water off it's only because the stream has turned cold, jolting him out of his trance. He steps out of the shower and finds water all over the bathroom floor. The shower curtain parts and the water splashes out onto the bathmat, and then the floor. Maybe the shower leaked as well. His clothes are soaked, and the water has seeped out into the lip of carpet under the door. "Goddamnit," Donnie says. There is no peace. Nothing is ever simple. He drops two more towels on the floor to cover the water and walks away.

He wraps himself in a towel and slogs out into the bedroom. He pulls on a pair of shorts and a red T-shirt. The room is so bright he almost needs sunglasses. Donnie is beginning to wish he was somewhere else.

In the kitchen Donnie finds a roll of garbage bags. He rips one from the tube and throws his soggy suit into it, grabs the shoes and socks and underwear that he was just wearing, and tosses them in the bag as well. He knots the bag, finds his key and heads down the stairwell once again. Donnie can feel the gritty concrete against the bottom of his feet. Sand, pebbles, grit.

Everything used to be so much better, Donnie thinks. He knows this is a common tune, but it's true. Nostalgia isn't an emotion, but a fact. Each and every year our society loses something of itself, Donnie thinks. Each and every year there are fewer and fewer reasons for living. Movie theaters are closing down. Book stores. Video stores. Record stores. Open land is converted to high-density town houses. Music has lost its moorings. Even the beach seems crowded and noisy compared to when my parents used to take me, Donnie thinks. He hates to be wistful, but he can't help how he feels.

Donnie walks through the parking garage to the Dumpster and throws his bag of clothes in the open slot, then turns around and walks back to the condo. But his bare feet chafe against the pavement and he stubs his toe. He curses himself. Bleeding, he sits on the curb where the mulch and the wall of the parking garage meet. The world revolves in puke green. Pure frustration. This is my absolute low point, Donnie thinks. This is it right here. He drops his forehead into the crook of his hands like an old cantaloupe, winces. Don't cry, he thinks, don't do that. Winces again.

As Donnie is sitting there holding his head in his hand, his toe bleeding onto the parking garage cement, he can hear the sounds of flip-flops slapping towards him. Schlup. Schlup. Schlup. Schlup. Then the sound of jingling keys next to his ear. He looks up to see Kevin, shirtless, face already red from the sun, a yellow and purple beach towel wrapped around his neck and shoulders like a stole. He grins ear to ear.

"Whadda ya sleeping down here?"

"Huh?" Donnie cocks his head between the recesses of his arms, peering up at Kevin's goofy smile. "I'm just—"

"Come on," Kevin says, jingling the keys. "Mom's making us hamburgers for lunch. And I'm starving." Kevin smacks his own face presses his hands to Donnie's head like a faith healer. "There, get some sun, boy. Whadda you been up to today anyway? I haven't seen you at all."

"I've been around," Donnie says. This is exactly what he needs: somebody to take him out of his shell. It's easy for me to get trapped in my mind, Donnie thinks. I should just spill it to Kevin. He'll twist it into a big joke. But then he's not sure if he's ready for that yet. Donnie lifts himself. Then Kevin tells him they should wrap that up before the sharks follow him up the shore. Kevin bends down and dabs the toe with his towel, and pretends to polish Donnie's invisible dress shoes.

"There," Kevin says. "That should keep you until we get upstairs."

Donnie nods. He wants to clasp his brother, thank him for understanding the dark marsh in which he is mired, and especially for avoiding calling attention to his state in the first place. Instead, Donnie limps towards the elevator and punches the up arrow.

"Can we take the elevator?"

"That'll make it harder on the sharks," Kevin says. Kevin almost bounces.

Kevin tells him about the volleyball friends, a couple of large families who came down together. Old friends.

"They seem so happy. I don't know if it's just me, but they seem happier than we are."

"Who?"

"Mom. Dad. Me. You. The family. I mean, we seem okay, but—"

"Yeah. But."

"You know what I mean?"

"Yeah. I've noticed," Donnie says. "It's off." He doesn't want to go further down that road. Donnie knows something is off-kilter, though he can't put his finger on it. But he can't do anything about it, can he? Might as well not worry about matters over which he has no control. He hasn't lost his head. Donnie turns the conversation back to Kevin. "Good group to hang out with?"

"Seems like it. It's nice to have something outside, you know."

"Yeah," Donnie says. It's almost as if Kevin's trying to tell him something. Again, he has to restrain his impulse from gut spilling. "Any girls?"

"Yeah," Kevin says. "All high school age though. Sorry."

"No problem."

"Yeah."

The elevator bings and Donnie feels the floor beneath him lift, the pulley system kick into place. His stomach curls within itself as the car rises.

Donnie watches the greasy hamburgers snap on the grill. A forked branch of blood dribbles from one. The six bundles of meat look like wallets. A dollop of fat pops onto the counter to the left of the burner. Donnie watches it harden in the air. The pink worms of flesh remind Donnie of the kind of oblong skin tags that his librarian in middle school used to have dangling from her neck like so many miniature turkey wattles. Always circling back to blemishes.

In addition to his waning appetite, Donnie no longer has a yen for a beach mole hunt. He wants to turn over a new leaf. Think positive. He wants something more from this trip than he initially expected. He wants to proceed forward without a thought in the opposite direction. He doesn't have to be so depressive and mopey, he thinks. So what if Janet is history? The Janets of this world are a dime a dozen. A nickel. There's got to be more to the beach than Hooters and saltwater taffy and sunburnt shoulders.

Kevin sits in the living room, flipping through the local newspaper. On the deck Donnie eyeballs the back of his father's head. His father sits staring out over the waves. His mother breezes into the kitchen, patting Donnie on the arm. She dries her hair with a towel, looking pensive for a moment. Then the moment is gone.

"Boy that quickie shower felt great," she says. "The ocean. It feels wonderful except for all that salt. If I don't wash it off. I'm like a sardine. You all should hop in after lunch."

"You make it sound so appealing, Mom," Kevin says.

Kevin helps her set the table and put hamburgers, potato chips, fruit, and spinach on the table. His mother places a loaf of bread and peanut butter next to Gary's plate. Donnie fills glasses with ice and water. Donnie wonders if his mother made hamburgers to get back at his father for yesterday. Maybe she was still annoyed at the fight they had after they went to bed. Donnie's father quit red meat years ago. She isn't usually vindictive, but then these small ruptures catch his eye. Perhaps he's not supposed to notice.

"Spinach?" Donnie asks her.

"Why not?"

They sit at the table. Ice cubes clink. Donnie feels the sweat on his glass of water ooze downward and he watches the chandelier swing in the air-conditioning. The chandelier resembles a jellyfish. The cedar dining room chairs are covered with baby blue upholstery and decorated with three vertical lines with horizontal squares cut into the wood.

His mother piles the hamburgers in a pyramid in the center of the table. Each burger is fringed with a ring skirt of onions and tomatoes, like chubby little ballerinas. Donnie's nose wrinkles at the luxuriant smell. Something about these burgers seems almost gamy to him today, overly fecund. The odor reminds him of mushroom rotting in the sun.

Kevin pushes a sliver of onion around his plate, chewing a large mouthful of burger. "What have you been up to all day, Dad?"

"Well. I woke up early in a sweat since your mother didn't want me running the air conditioning. I took a walk along the beach at around 5:30 and watched all the idiots out there flying kites like children, and jogging in their idiotic shorts. I walked back to the condo and almost broke my back in the pool of vomit some low life drunkard spewed in our stairwell. Then I holed myself up for the rest of the day, cleansing myself in the bedroom and praying while your mother was out there basking like a beached whale."

Silverware clinking.

"Sounds nice," Kevin says.

Donnie's mother swallows her bite of hamburger. She breathes deeply and sighs. Donnie wants to tell her of his breathing exercises.

"Gary. This is our vacation. Jesus Christ."

"Oh, no you don't. Don't you *ever* say His name in that way," he barks.

At this he stands up, reaches into the bowl of fruit and pulls out an apple. Holding his glass of water and his peanut butter sandwich in one hand and an apple in the other, Donnie's father walks back into the bedroom, softly clicks the door shut.

Donnie stares at the untouched bowl of spinach and feels guilty for the work his mother put into the meal. He spoons himself a small pile and thinks of the seaweed woman in the beach shop. That's what I mean about unexplored territory, he thinks. Worth seeking out. That's something at least. Donnie stares at the wall.

This could be a disaster, Donnie thinks. He's kicking along the edge of the water. The waves lick at his feet, and several tug him into the softer sand. But he picks at the shards of shells tumbling onto the harder sand. Is it low tide or high tide? Why do shells litter the beach now when often only sand is visible? Donnie feels out of his element, ignorant of the mechanics of what surrounds him. It's not as if I'm smooth, or well equipped to approach them, Donnie thinks. These girls. These women. I don't even know who she is. I haven't even seen her face. Curiosity can lead to a quick disgrace.

Donnie bends down over a small, purplish-white shell. It looks worn, tossed in wave after wave. He thinks it's an oyster shell, but he's not sure. I can't believe this is the first complete shell I've seen, Donnie thinks. Another reason to believe the world is going to hell in a hand basket: where *are* all the shells? When he was a kid Donnie remembers finding shells littering the beach. He has that lampshade at home filled with them. Now you are lucky to find fragments. It must be a parallel to the snowstorm situation, he thinks. When is the last time we've seen a decent blizzard? Ten years ago. It has to be connected. He slips the shell into his back pocket.

This time Donnie doesn't want to rush right in the store like an unhinged zealot. He stands outside and thinks. How should I do this? What is the right approach? He looks at the façade of the store: white stucco-looking material (fake stucco?)

with the Sun Store emblazoned in yellow and orange across the entrance. The screen porch clacks in the wind. A fly bounces in the opening. It's amazing what you *don't* notice, Donnie thinks. He wonders how many otherworldly details he's missed when he was caught up in his endless thought-stream.

Donnie walks into the shop. He meanders through the aisles of beach paraphernalia, but he doesn't see a sign of seaweed woman. Odd. For a moment Donnie wonders if he imagined her. "Jack and Diane" is playing idly on the overhead speakers. He failed to notice the speakers last time. He also didn't notice the giant sun mural painted on the rear wall or the rays that exude from it in mustard stripes. Then he spots the stubby burnt woman who accosted him earlier. At least *she's* not imaginary. Chin propped in hand, she sits behind the counter reading a celebrity magazine.

"Hi," Donnie says. "How are you?"

"Fine. Can I help you?"

Donnie smooths his shirt with one flat hand. "I was actually in here earlier. I'm looking for the woman I saw on the floor putting price tags on the plastic shovels."

The woman squinches her face and smacks a fly away from her head. She peers back into her magazine, as if some eternal revelation is about to be divulged.

"You must mean Jo," she says. "Friend?"

"Acquaintance, more or less," Donnie says.

"She's on her lunch break. Take a look down the boardwalk." Scratching her forehead, the woman doesn't look up.

"The boardwalk?"

"Uh-huh," the woman says.

"And when will she return from her break?"

At this she *does* snap away from her fashion photos. "What's it to you?"

"Gotcha. Right. Thanks. I'll try the boardwalk." Donnie starts for the door, before he finds himself in a position where he has to *explain* himself.

"Hey, if you see her tell her not to forget my fries. She can be very, you know, forgetful." She says this as if she's sending a warning to Donnie. But it only endears her to him even more. Forgetful. He can handle forgetful. Forgetful is folksy. What he can't handle is anything in the uptight realm. What that is he's still trying to discern, but the distinction has to be made, Donnie thinks.

He steps from the Sun Shop into the sun.

Donnie walks up and down the short boardwalk looking for the seaweed woman. He spots old men pushing their grandchildren in strollers, couples swinging hands, and teenage girls in skimpy bathing suits. He averts his eyes from any and all moles. The benches and small shops are mostly empty at this time of day. A few kids eating ice cream out of garishly decorated paper cups. Couples wolfing down fries. No sign of Jo anywhere. The biting sense of loss balls up within him. He's ready to throw in the towel already.

Just as Donnie is about to give up, Jo cuts from the funnel cake stand directly in front of his path. The funnel cake teeters on a greasy paper plate in her left hand, and she holds a cup of fries in the other and she glides to the closest bench. Confectionary sugar speckles the top of her hand. Donnie stops in his tracks. Suddenly it's as if he just realizes he's at the *beach*, as if the world around him was on sensory mute until this moment. A flood of smells, sounds, and sights slides towards Donnie at this moment—the salt air, the seagulls circling overhead, the screams of children, the thrum of waves and the hissing withdraw, the smell of grease, and French fries, and pizza, the smell of hot tar from the boardwalk pillars, his dry cracked lips. He watches Jo as she hunches and dangles a ribbon of funnel cake over her mouth and lets it drop onto her tongue.

For a minute Donnie watches Jo eat without notice, then she glances up at him and looks away. Then she glances up at him and turns away in disgust. Then she turns her body to face the sea. He continues to stare, and she turns away. At this point Donnie approaches. This time he doesn't see any evidence of seaweed though.

Before he even reaches the bench Jo snaps her head and says: "Hey, do you have a problem?"

"Probably," he says. "That's probably true."

"I don't know you, do I?"

From his new, closer perspective, Donnie realizes how gawky and off-key this woman actually is. He's guessing she's twenty-five, twenty-six, but she has a sort of lazy left eye, and an odd, asymmetrical paunch congests around her ribs. Her posture is horrible: she leans to the left side, with a sort of odd bestial tilt, reminding Donnie of a hulking dinosaur—legs out of proportion to her torso. Her one good eye is vulnerable, but simultaneously steeled and wary.

"I'm sorry. I owe you an apology," Donnie says. "I was actually in the store earlier today, and—"

"What store?" Jo squints into the sun. Donnie wonders how someone who works at the beach can step outside without sunglasses. Perhaps they get used to the glare? The afternoon shadows are beginning to leak onto the gray boardwalk from the railing and lifeguard towers. Seagulls caw overhead and Donnie can see sandpipers race the waves.

"The Sun Shop."

"Oh. Right," she says.

"Right. And, well. I was the one wearing the suit this morning. I don't think you saw me."

Jo covers her mouth. Most likely stifling a snicker, Donnie thinks. But he doesn't see her mouth crease. "What were you doing in a suit? You mean a suit-suit, right?"

"Right. I don't know," Donnie says. "I feel lost."

Jo doesn't have much to say to this, and in the encroaching silence Donnie listens to the radio static radiating from the funnel cake stand. He wonders if she's going to ask him why he feels lost, but she pushes another strand of funnel cake in her mouth instead.

"You were putting stickers on plastic shovels this morning," Donnie continues.

"Yeah, that's right. You really are quite observational."

"Do you...I mean, have you worked there for a long time?"

"Well, that's not a very interesting question. I mean, is it? Instead of answering that one, how 'bout I elaborate on the shovels?"

"Okay."

"Take a seat," she says, lifting herself to the left to make room. Donnie sits next to her, resting his hands stiff on his lap, as if he were in a formal Victorian portrait.

"Thanks."

"See, the thing is, I can actually carry on about plastic shovels. It sounds insipid, but I actually think they are beautiful. That's when you were at the shop—when I was in a sort of shovel trance, you might say."

"I don't get—"

"Well, I think of them as, like, gifts from an alien planet. They have those perfect curves. And the colors are magnificent if you take the time to look at them. That's the thing. They are molded and sculpted, and I know they are identical but they are also unique in their own way to me."

"Hmm."

"Most people are in a rush to get their suntan lotion or T-shirt. They don't notice

The little things."

"That's an interesting point," Donnie says. "So, is that what you're into—shovels?"

"No, oh jeez. It's almost two. Hillary is going to can me if I don't get back."

Jo wipes her fingers on a wad of napkins, picks up the cup of fries and chucks the paper plate in the trashcan. Something about the gesture reminds Donnie of his brother. Not a bad association. She is not an unappealing woman, Donnie thinks.

"Come on to the store if you want. I'll show you a thing or two."

As Donnie stands up he notices a teenage boy feeding blue cotton candy to his black Labrador. The seagulls circle overhead for handouts.

In the shade of the Sun Store Jo points out the shells to Donnie, telling him about each one. Donnie asks her about the seaweed. She says it must have been from the early morning. She tells him the things she does before the sun dares to crack the surface of the horizon: collecting shells, picking driftwood from the breakers, sifting through the post-storm flotsam and jetsam for whatever might wash up, soaking in the emptiness before it's corrupted, staring into the wide lightening line encircling her vision. She tells Donnie of these things with a steady neutrality, an almost apathetic tone. Yet Donnie notices her keen immediacy. He can tell she has layers upon layers. He's glad the burnt woman lets them be.

Jo holds up a thin elongated shell that reminds Donnie of stuffed manicotti or a small snake that swallowed an egg. The speakers are playing ambient techno. The music is present but almost invisible.

"Take this, for instance," she says. "You ever see one of *these* around the beach?"

"No. I've never—"

"That's because they're not around here," she whispers. "This one's probably from Australia or New Guinea. They kill the mollusk inside, bleach them out. But it's picturesque. Beautiful. Tourists eat these up. They are exotic, you know." Her mouth is pursed into an O at this, and she turns away, perhaps embarrassed. Donnie can feel her brain churning, processing his sudden presence in her life, how it fits into some new shifting order. She's a woman who is conscious of alternatives, a true sign of a free spirit. He doesn't know many true free spirits. His own spirit is quite shackled, he knows, more than it needs to be.

Jo points to more shells on the shelf and informs Donnie

that most of them aren't from Delaware or Maryland or anywhere nearby for that matter. She says as far as shells are concerned around here you have to really dig for the best ones.

"You need to get off the beach itself for the most part. And early."

Jo says she can show him. Donnie says he's up for that if she'll go.

"Tomorrow?" Donnie nods, noticing the pink flakes of singed something at the base of the shelf. Jo smells faintly of cinnamon. He guesses it's the residue from some sort of aromatherapy. "The only reason I'm inviting you, though…I can tell you're a sensitive guy who thinks about things. I would never take some frat boy who is just after a lay. You're not some wacko are you? I'm not going to end up chopped up into bits in a garbage bag." Donnie thinks of his bag of soggy clothes. Donnie smiles and gives her the thumbs-up.

"Say around four thirty. I'll come by to get you. Just tell me where you're staying."

Donnie pulls out an old gas receipt from his shorts pocket, scribbles down The Bluff, room 417 around back. He tells her she needs a pass to get through the gates, that they have security guards. "They are on the lookout for young shell collectors," Donnie says. She shrugs.

"Don't worry so much," she says.

"Okay," Donnie says. "I'll try not to." Donnie has a hunch something worthwhile might spring from all of this, though he can't be sure.

"Okay." She motions to the back of the store, says she needs to return to work: responsibilities, duty, and obligation. Donnie nods and backs out of the store. The drum machine underlay melds with the threshing sound of surf. Donnie can feel both ripple in his stomach.

Donnie has always enjoyed cooking. Even when he was a young child learning to make lasagna from his mother, there was something calming about it. The thought of using life to continue life sedates his impulses. So when he returns to the condo he's in a cooking mood. Nothing fancy; just the process is enough.

On the cutting board Donnie slices mushrooms, onions, green peppers, tomatoes, and tosses them in a bowl with lettuce, oil, and vinegar. Pepper. Parmesan cheese. He husks corn and boils it. He fries chicken covered in ground cornflakes. He grates red potatoes and sautés the hash with garlic and onion. His mother tries to convince him to add more cheese or milk, some kind of dairy. But Donnie shakes his head without engaging her in a long drawn-out affair. She's obsessed with osteoporosis. Her words.

Donnie sends Kevin to knock on the bedroom door, where his father has locked himself in. No answer. His mother sets the table and Donnie serves the hash browns and chicken and places the salad and corn on the table. Donnie, Kevin, and their mother sit at the table watching the sky darken, the ever-present hiss of the ocean as a backdrop. Gary doesn't emerge from the bedroom. They talk about Kevin's volleyball games, and the school of dolphins their mother saw. She says she ran along the beach, following them for twenty minutes. "Boy, that was something," she says.

They finish eating and Donnie scoops the rest of the hash browns and two chicken thighs on his plate. He doles out a bowl full of salad for his father. As they are cleaning up, Gary silently scuffles to his seat and eats—stabbing into his lettuce as if it insulted him. He tears into the chicken with his incisors, like a wild dog. Kevin elbows Donnie to watch.

"So, Dad," Donnie says. "I was wondering if Kevin and I could use the car tonight. We want to—"

"No."

"We just want to—"

"Where to?"

"Just drive around the—"

"You're not just driving around aimlessly. In my car."

"No, we just—"

"I'll go with you then," he says.

His father seems to either ignore him or treat him as if he was still a child. He is an adult, but not an adult. Donnie objects, but his father is in a state. Donnie can't access his father anymore. He is the "voice of authority."

Kevin says he'll just stay in and watch television instead.

"Yeah, I'm definitely going," Gary says. "I want to see this 'driving around.'"

Donnie watches his father, shoulders hunched, pushing the hash browns onto his fork with his fingers. He doesn't look up until every thin scrap of food is eaten. Sometimes Donnie thinks of himself as a muddy puddle. A stagnant quality hangs over his life: ripples only transpire when someone else throws a pebble. It's a slow, passive, reactionary sort of life. But watching his father eat makes him realize the old man has it worse somehow. I pity him, Donnie thinks. If that's possible. He seems controlled by some foreign impulse, at odds with his true nature, a victim of parasites beyond his vision.

Donnie wants to drive but his father is not hearing any part of it. His father reminds him that the last time Donnie drove the car he momentarily fell asleep behind the wheel and nearly ran off the road. How he came upon that knowledge is a mystery to Donnie though. Donnie slumps in the passenger seat and his father turns the ignition. They pull out onto the strip.

"So, where are we going, exactly?"

Donnie points north, and his father drives in that direction. Donnie rolls his window down to smell the ocean breeze, but his father tells him to roll it back up. His allergies. Too humid. Air-conditioning.

"So, we're just driving north with no particular destination?"

"Yeah," Donnie says. He doesn't understand why his father is blowing this out of proportion. Cruising the beach isn't all that unusual, he thinks, even if his intentions are simply to escape, to be anywhere but there. Aren't vacations *about* escape? It's a typical thing to do. "Just driving around, you know."

His father winces at that, fingering the air-conditioning vent.

"Why are you such a *drifter*?"

Donnie shakes his head. He can't believe he's getting a lecture, on vacation, at his age, on such a trivial topic.

"You don't seem to have any enthusiasm at all. To do anything. No drive." He glowers at Donnie "What's with you?"

"I'm drifting, but I'm drifting *toward* something, Dad. It may not appear that way. I don't know. Didn't you do that when you were young?"

His father ignores that. "What then? What are you

drifting toward?" Donnie hears how his father knew exactly what he wanted at sixteen. It wasn't a grand mystery. It wasn't some self-indulgent 'search.' It just was. Just like an oak tree just is an oak tree. Donnie spins the air-conditioning vent away from his face.

"I don't know yet. You know, I'm...trying to uncover that."

His father sighs and blows a puff of air at the dashboard. The sun fades beyond the horizon and the streetlamps flutter. Traffic is heavy on the strip, and Donnie watches the cars and restaurants and hotels glide by. Miniature golf joints with pirate themes and video game huts blinking with lights. Salt water taffy. T-shirt shops. Donuts. Donnie's father pulls into the left lane.

"Where are we going?" Donnie asks.

"The bumper car place," he says, pointing over his shoulder. A grin rises on his face. "How about it, kiddo?"

It's not merely hypocrisy, Donnie thinks. His father's so-called spiritual side rarely rears its head except in its designated place. He seems able to segregate his fatherly and Godly duties altogether, and it's not an even match. Donnie runs his finger down the window, and his father hands him a handkerchief from his pocket, and points at the streak. Donnie nods and wipes the streak clean, and hands the handkerchief back to his father without looking.

The electricity crackles overhead and the sheer, silvery surface of the floor glimmers under the lights: Donnie feel as if he's about to be executed, operated upon by aliens. Something cold and antiseptic. Bring it on, he thinks. If my father is off-key enough to lug me here to resurrect his youth, I'm crazy enough to deny it to him.

His father sneers at the steering wheel. Next to him in a green and white striped car, Donnie shrugs. Why does everything have to be so complicated and competitive? He seems to bristle with this sense of doom, Donnie thinks. It just makes him edgy being around his father.

The short tomboy with dyed red hair running the bumper cars presses the buzzer, and suddenly Donnie is bumped from all sides. A kid with spiky blonde hair rams him several times from behind, thrusting Donnie towards a pile-up of yellow and silver cars in the center of the floor. But Donnie jerks the wheel to the right and knocks a pregnant woman in a purple car, spinning her ninety degrees. She laughs and moves on to the right. Donnie steers away from his father, who is bashing a teenage girl's white car into the far right wall.

Just then Donnie catches his father's backward glance and Gary pulls off the girl. Donnie circles a clump of bashing cars in the center of the floor, but his father tails him, then heads around the pileup in the opposite direction. He can feel the revulsion pulsating from his father. Donnie knows he's not imaging that. Yet, Donnie can't easily buy into his father's aggression: this coming from one of God's so-called servants.

The impact jolts Donnie's neck first, a rippling shudder that sends his car smashing into the far wall. The rubberized bumper is pressed into the wall as Gary rams Donnie's car over and over, jostling Donnie's head again and again. Within the noise and thumping music, Donnie can hear his father saying, "Now what will you do? Now what will you do? I got you now!" Donnie closes his eyes and lets it happen. Over and over.

Before Donnie can peel off the wall and initiate a

counter-attack, another car joins his father's assault, creating a wedge. Ultimately Donnie breathes a sigh of relief as the jolting slows, and then the buzzer buzzes again and the throbbing halts.

As his father drives home, Donnie sits staring at the dashboard. He watches his father's fingers knead the grooves in the steering wheel. His father flips the air-conditioner on and breathes deeply. Perhaps this will make things better, Donnie thinks. If he feels release, that's good. If so, I'll be a rag doll every time. Short term, it can't hurt. The long run is all that matters, he thinks. He heaves his head back into the seat.

Sunday

Donnie has a dream that he's a blind child. He makes a papier-mâché doll in school, and he becomes attached to it. He sleeps with the doll and eats with the doll. Before school one day his father tells him boys shouldn't bring dolls to school and he takes the doll away from him. Donnie makes another doll, the same as the first.

Donnie wakes up in a sweat to the sound of rain on the roof. And then thunder. He drifts back to sleep, and wakes again to the sound of light knocking at the front door. Jo. Donnie pulls on a pair of shorts and a T-shirt and grabs his flip-flops from the deck. Jo raps the door again lightly. He listens to hear if anybody else stirs. He doesn't hear a thing. He opens the door.

Jo stands dressed in black pants and a navy blue windbreaker with a bucket in her hand and a backpack on one shoulder. A baseball cap is pulled tightly over her head, shading her eyes until she lifts them, blinking in the foyer light. Then her eyes dart over Donnie's face.

"You're not going to be comfortable like that," she says in a husky whisper.

"No?"

"No. It's cold out there. We're going to be catching most of the incoming gusts. Plus it rained last night. Go put some pants on and grab a sweatshirt," she says.

"Right on. Be right back," Donnie whispers. "Just wait here."

Even though Jo's minor bossiness at this moment reminds him of Janet, Donnie realizes that he's not as sexually interested in this woman as he was the day before. At first he thought he was—she was still vague and dim. A mere idea. Now that she's becoming clearer, his lower half has lost interest. Donnie is pleased by this. Donnie knows he's wish-washy—and overly sensitive. But Janet still did a number on him. She wasn't exactly empathetic, he thinks. But then again, rawness has taken over at the gut level.

He dresses in what Jo requests—sweatshirt, jeans—but when he returns he can't find her. He looks at the bathroom door—open. He looks at the deck—empty. He looks in the living room—dark. Then he hears a door creak, and the door to his parents' room opens. Jo walks out. He can't believe it. What the hell does she think she's doing? At this Donnie waves her out of the condo and snaps the door shut.

"What are you—"

"Hold on. I was just looking around that's all. I didn't wake anybody. It's fine."

"But that's my parents'—"

"Yeah, they look sweet sleeping there. Her arm was sort

of wrapped around his neck. I'm sorry. Look, I have a thing for watching people. It's just fascinating to me."

Donnie doesn't know what to say. So he doesn't say a thing.

"You don't like to watch?"

"No, I meant the *position* my parents are in." Donnie tells her how his parents used to sleep in separate beds, and still do from time to time. He imagined them isolated to their individual sides of the bed.

Donnie thinks of a thousand possible rebuttals to Jo's action: invasion, overstepping boundaries, breach of trust, breach of guest etiquette. But then he realizes that it's small potatoes, not worth pursuing. He digs his hands in his pockets.

"Let's go find some shells," Donnie says.

"You'll need some old tennis shoes too," she says. "Don't want your feet to get too scraped up. It can be sharp." Donnie does what he is told.

Jo drives them over the same stretch of highway that Donnie and his father just covered the night before. Only this time the street is empty. The lights are green. Above the haze of streetlamps faint stars throb. She drives away and out of the strip of fast food restaurants and bars, and into a dark swath of dunes, brush, and road illuminated by the headlights of her Honda Civic. This is the kind of place where people get whacked, Donnie thinks. For a moment he entertains the passing sensational thought that Janet hired Jo to eliminate him. Patently absurd. The wind gusts and Jo holds the steering wheel with both hands to steady the car.

"How far are we going?" Donnie wonders, watching the

ominous landscape scroll by. Of course, considering her proclivity for spying, Donnie thinks she could be kidnapping him.

"Up the promontory—the mud flats up there are prime." She talks like a man, Donnie thinks. No verbiage. Nothing wasted. There's something to this, he thinks. This is good.

Eventually she turns onto a narrow gravel road to the right, leading through junipers and heather and ending at a circle driveway abutting a green ramshackle shack on a bluff overlooking the ocean. Jo cuts the ignition and steps out of the car, slinging her bucket and backpack. The rain has stopped, but Jo was right about the wind. Donnie quickly slings his sweatshirt on and ties the hood around his head. As they walk past the house, Donnie notices the jumble of boxes and black trash bags on the porch. A light is on in the far corner of the structure, but Donnie doesn't see any movement. Jo walks away from the house, down a path leading to the beach.

"I thought we're heading to mud flats," Donnie says.

"We are. We have to walk to them. No access from the road."

As they descend the dunes the sand whips up in the wind and scours Donnie's face. He turns his head and sidles down until he slips and hunches from the wind and picks himself up and follows Jo with his head tilted upward toward the waning stars. Jo beelines without flinching.

"Don't worry," she says, without turning. "Once we're along the water the wind will just basically spray us. This is the worst of it."

"Okay."

She doesn't say a word about the house or where they are

headed, much less how long it might take to get there. Donnie picks up the pace to let her body shield him from the wind as they approach the breakers.

Once they reach the edge of the water the gusts pick up, but Jo is right—it is thankfully devoid of scouring sand. They turn left along the water and walk paralleling the wrack line, the spray from the ocean fuming at intervals, giving Donnie the impression of riding a boat *through* the waves rather than walking along them. The waves rear and crash with a wild hammering thrush. As they walk and the sky lightens Donnie watches the waves peak, trickling froths of foam as they descend then whirl forward, thumping into the surf and exploding up the beach.

"The storm is still off coast," Jo says. "My bet is the waves will be very rough all day."

"Great." Jo bends over a clump of driftwood, seaweed, and pebbles, and pulls at a string of what looks like chips.

"Even better for shelling. Yeah. Watch your feet as we're going. The beach usually doesn't have much to offer here, but with this storm we might have some surprises along the wrack line."

Jo unzips her backpack and withdraws a large flashlight, flips it on. She points the beam at her clenched fingers and opens them slowly.

"Whelk egg cases," she says. "Tiny. Pretty." She holds them up for Donnie to see. He watches the translucent shells, the size of corn kernels, some just cuticles and broken shards. They spin in the wind like a whirly-gig. Jo smiles and places the small nursery back where she found it.

"We're almost there," she says, handing him the bucket.

"Make yourself *useful*. Put a little salt water in there, if you would." As he passes her—shivering, bending over the froth for a covering of water—she play-punches him on the shoulder and leads the way along the beach, weaving and bobbing among the debris.

"We're going in there?" Donnie asks. Jo's flashlight illuminates a vast muddy expanse to the left of the cape, peppered with gulls and the murmur of flies. The sky is bright enough that Donnie can see the brute facts: the dense slop of sand and sludge, littered with lighter patches—shells and debris, he guesses. But the smell hits hardest: a reeking odor of ooze, and brine, rotting crabs and jellyfish, a brooding funk singed with the sharpness of death. The wind halts here, as if it too is fearful.

"Of course," Jo says. "Watch your feet though. Put this over your mouth if you want. Maybe roll up your pants if you don't want them covered in slime." She tosses Donnie a bandana from her backpack and tells him that if he'll hold the bucket she'll manage the shovel and flashlight for now. And with that Jo forges ahead (no bandana, pants unrolled).

"See why I thought you should wear sneakers?"

Jo sludges through the mud about fifteen feet, then points her flashlight at her feet to the left. Donnie follows. At each step he can hear the shluck, shluck, shluck of the mud and water. Jo stops. At this she squats and slowly sinks her shovel into the muck, then pivots the handle of the shovel in it and lifts the contents just as slowly to the surface, keeping the flashlight steady upon the point of entry. In the wash of flashlight to the right Donnie can make out a handful of herring gulls stamping on a swash bar at the tip of the spit. He wonders if they are searching for food. Jo wobbles the shovel lightly and pokes through it with her finger, shaking loose clumps of mud from it.

"Reach into my backpack and grab the sieve, would you? Be careful of the knife and pick. Don't jab yourself."

Donnie feels around in the cluttered backpack— something plastic and round, something pointy, something flat and pockmarked like a window screen. That must be it. He zips open the flaps and withdraws a flat, rusty strainer with large wooden handles, careful not to let the contents of the backpack spill out. Jo dumps the contents of her shovel onto the mesh, and shakes it briskly. The water drips through. The mud clumps and she breaks each one with her fingers, and then flips it at her feet. A glassy looking tube, a small, motionless pink jellyfish, a tangle of seaweed, a crab's claw, and three shells.

"Let me see that bucket," she says.

Jo flicks the seaweed, the claw and the jellyfish back into the mud, and she drops the tube and the shells into the bucket, leaving the shovel in the muck and probing her flashlight into the water within the bucket.

"Waterproof," she says.

"What is that tube thing?" Donnie wonders.

"It's just the tip of a worm casing. A tube worm," she says. "I probably scared it good, and the worm retreated below. Those things can run for several feet. That's what those gulls are doing over there—except they're trying to get them to the surface. Different kind of worm."

Donnie asks about the shells, and she says one is a dwarf tellins, but it's alive and she doesn't need any more at home. Donnie doesn't fully understand, but decides not to ask. Jo plucks it out of the bucket and sets it gently back down in the muck. The second one is a detached false angel wing, which she says are pretty common, but since it's a nice sample she says she'd like to hold onto it. The large round one is a shell called a shark eye, but she's not sure if the snail is inside or not. "I don't take live ones unless I can *keep* them alive." She tilts the shell carefully upside down and peers inside, and doesn't find anybody home. She places it back at the bottom of the bucket, careful not to jostle the shell.

"This is what it's all about," she says. "You don't know what you're going to find on any given day."

Jo steps forward, and Donnie follows, slapping his arm from the biting flies and gnats that zip into his ears.

As the sky continues to brighten and open up, the musky shadings of the mud flat reveal themselves to Donnie and the bucket of seawater fills with both shells and living mollusks. Donnie's mindset parallels the rising tide. He feels a sudden widening of possibilities, a sense that daily reality isn't as dismal as he makes it out to be sometimes. He follows Jo's lead through the murk, digs in hard, like earthworms aerating a field. Jo talks in a dull muted voice as she sifts the mud and shells over the sieve, and Donnie says hardly a word. He feels he's at the end of the earth, or on some newly discovered planet. The sun strikes the cape in a triangular wedge, and the caw of gulls rises as if to meet it.

With this Jo leads Donnie out of the mud flat and out onto the beach itself, wringing her soggy pants legs out with her fingers. Donnie removes his muddy shoes and toes the cool sand beneath his feet. He can hear the shells shift in the bucket and the movement of small living creatures. Jo methodically packs the instruments of their search in her backpack and they meander back towards the surf and sandpipers dancing among it.

Donnie tells her he's glad she asked him to come along, and she nods and says she was apprehensive he'd become grossed out by the stench, and that there are only so many people who will go to this length for a few bits of calcium, but that she's pleased he came. She tells Donnie's she's been collecting shells for over ten years and that she doesn't know what she would do without the hobby, that it's been a solace through the death of her mother two years ago and her father's flight to Oregon to try to reconcile the loss. Rudderless. Jo glances out into the surf, wincing at the glare evolving on the horizon.

"After the past few years I'm just starting to, you know, to put my life back in a direction it should be going. I was paralyzed for so long after she died. I just felt I had so much to do, but in actuality I didn't. It was a simple matter that I made complicated. I just felt too *human*."

Donnie puts his hand on her shoulder and leaves it there, and she doesn't object, and they continue walking like that. Jo kicks the sand up and they angle towards the water. She allows her feet to hug the surf, so it might dilute the mud, and cool the fly bites on her feet. She explains this.

"I could be microscopic. Sometimes I wish I was. I mean, it's a whole world down there that's different and complex. But it's not the kind of complexity that gives us problems. It's more manageable."

Jo says that when she was a girl growing up in the suburbs of Philadelphia she was always fixated on examining the dirt. She would go into the backyard with a magnifying glass, and just sort through whatever she could find—insects, bits of rock, the tiniest roots. She could get lost.

"This is what people need," she says. "Something outside of themselves to stay balanced."

Donnie nods and lets his arm drop, and asks her what time she has to work, and she says nine, but that it's only six thirty. He is stunned at the insight. She is completely right.

"Let's get some breakfast," she says. And they walk on. She walks, he follows.

In the daylight Donnie thinks the shack looks worse than it did under the shadow of darkness. The entire left side of the façade sags under the weight of the roof. The wooden siding is bleached and warped from the sun and salt air, and in desperate need of replacing. The back porch is missing floorboards, and several gashes mar the screen mesh. As they trudge up the dunes, Donnie watches a small bird dart in and out of a gap above the back door. He can see two figures standing close together behind the thin sheath of curtain in the kitchen window.

Jo leads him up into the porch, telling him to watch his step on both sides—"stay to the middle," she says—and she drops her backpack in the corner of the porch and knocks on the back door. The entrance smells of citronella candles, and he can hear the distinct done of flies or mosquitoes. No wonder they don't have chairs out here, Donnie thinks. Too bad. Donnie hears a slow scraping movement inside, and the door jerks open, as if in irritation.

"Hi, Helen. Hi, Grant."

In the dusty shadows of the interior, Donnie can see the

old couple, hip to hip, huddling against each other, both wearing sunglasses. They both clear their throats, almost in tandem, and they shuffle forward, stopping at the rotten molding, inches from Jo.

The man cranes his neck forward, and licks his lips. "Jo, is that you?" The woman cranes her neck forward, and licks her dry lips.

"Yes. Yes. But I have a guest with me. This is my new friend, Donnie."

"Oh," they both say at once. "Well, that's fine. Come on in, you two." They scuffle away from the door, propelling dust motes in their wake. Jo closes the door behind her, and the couple scuffs forward through the hall, clutching each other. The sun angles through the upper half of each curtained window. The effect: the ceiling is enlightened, but the rest of the house is muted in a sepia haze. The lighting makes Donnie think of a disco, or a trendy bar. Sheer accident.

Donnie follows Jo through the living room, cluttered with more stacks of boxes, decorated only with a faded circular throw rug. Two love seats are shoved together in the center of the room, though both are covered with papers in disarray. They walk through a short hallway layered with florid wallpaper and worn in a pattern around arm level. The kitchen is the brightest and cleanest room with an extension on the far side where a table holds more cardboard boxes pressed against the window. However, the windows facing the sea are all unobstructed, and the sunlight surges into the room from them.

"Please sit down," the woman says. Donnie and Jo both sit at the kitchen table, and Grant whispers to Helen.

"Oh, go ahead and move those boxes, Jo. You can put

them in the living room if you like." Jo nods and motions for Donnie to stay. She lifts the boxes and balances them with her right hand, stumbling into the living room. Aside from their age and evident blindness, the sort of complicit secrecy that the old couple maintains strikes Donnie. With them everything seems to be a code of gestures, motions and murmurs. Helen turns to the stove and Grant clings to her. He dumps the contents of a small bowl into the pan, and breaks an egg into a pan, then another, then another, and with a groan Helen bends over and turns the dial to the front burner, and lifts a wooden spoon and begins stirring the eggs in the pan.

"How about some food, Jo?" She pivots her body slightly at the thought. Jo walks back into the room, and points at Donnie for confirmation. Donnie nods.

"Sure, Helen. Do you need any help over there?"

"No, I've got my helper here at my side," she says. Grant nods, and cracks another egg in the pan. That's the truth, Donnie thinks. This is contrary to everything I'm accustomed to, he knows.

The plate that Helen hands Donnie is heaped with a mound of eggs scrambled with bits of olive, tomatoes, and cream cheese abutting two wedges of dark bread. She plunks a pitcher of water on the table, and Jo pulls glasses from the cupboard near the window. Helen and Grant lumber to the table and Jo pulls out their chairs despite the protests.

"She's such a good daughter, isn't she?"

He looks at Jo, who averts her eyes, and stands for napkins, and sits down with a pile of them. She passes them around the table, and Donnie pierces with his fork.

"Daughter?" Donnie murmurs. At this Jo kicks his shin,

and he notices that Helen and Grant are bent in prayer, and he drops his fork and bends his head too, and feels immediately guilty. Grant clears his throat and speaks in a hushed mumble: "God, thank you for your gifts, and for blessing for this food. Amen."

As they begin eating, Grant and Helen tell Jo about their driftwood findings on the beach. Grant is a driftwood artist, Jo explains. The contents of the boxes are mostly filled with his driftwood sculptures and the morning after a storm is the best time to find unique pieces. Helen nods and speaks of their need to maintain some order in their lives, even at their age. Even in their condition.

"Donnie, we're both eighty four years old," she says. "And at our age we can't do much without each other, not well. As you probably noticed, we're pretty much inseparable."

"I see," Donnie says. He rips a mouthful of bread from the mass. The bread is a dense pumpernickel of some sort, with an odor of seaweed and salt. "What attracted you to driftwood?"

Grant bobs his head in confusion, and Helen grasps his hand on the table, then pats his head. He looks as if it is a strain to simply find the words. "It's all around us," he says. "It's here, everywhere." Helen kisses his forehead, and he nods with a slight grin. Donnie thinks that he's grinning more at the idea than the fact that he found the words for it.

Jo raises her eyebrows and says that Grant is good enough to sell his work to local stores, including The Sunshine Store. It brings them a small income, she tells him, gives them something to do out here. Grant bends forward and points at the window and the water dazzling in the sunshine over the dunes, and the birds squawking over them.

"What's here is here for a reason. Young man, I'm sure you are aware of the old free will debate. The determinism side versus the belief that we control our actions."

"Yes, sir," Donnie says.

"Well, of course, this missed the point. The point is that we are put on this earth to be guardians of a sort. You know that I'm sure."

"No, I'm not," Donnie says. "What do you mean?"

"Guardians. Guardians of that which we are surrounded by. We live here on this shelf of land because we are meant to care for it. We look out for it. But also because we are *meant* to. There is something beyond us that we have to heed or we'd be guilty of kicking sand in His face."

Donnie asks if they are talking about a calling.

"Yes. That's right." He slaps his lips together. Liver spots adorn his face and hands, and yet Donnie can see an image of Grant in his youth saying the same things. He's holding on.

"Exactly. That's exactly right," he says. "A calling."

As they finish eating, Grant and Helen rise and collect the dishes, and pile them in the sink, and say that they have many things to do today. This isn't what Donnie expected. How many things can a driftwood sculptor and his wife have to do? But then they live here, and he's on a family vacation. It's all relative. He nods at Jo and she says they should leave. But as they are making their way for the door Helen says they should come over for dinner, and to see some of the sculptures, and that they'd be more than welcome, and Donnie finds himself saying yes, yes, yes, though he isn't sure why.

"Bye Mom, bye Dad," Jo says, and then they back out into the conflagration of sunshine.

As Jo carefully wedges the shells in the space where the front and back seats meet, and drives Donnie back past the dunes and brush, and back into the strip, gleaming in the early morning sun, Donnie thinks of the intense intimacy Helen and Grant share, their symbiotic relationship. He wonders if they were always this way or if their condition made them so, and he asks Jo. He hopes he isn't over-romanticizing. She shakes her head and says it's a pity, and that they found themselves both going nearly blind at the same time. "Pure coincidence," she says. Donnie watches the tendons at the back of her neck, and the slope of her shoulder and thinks she's a good person, and that she seems finer in the light of day than she did in the dusk, and that it's a good sign, isn't it?

"I was wondering," Donnie says, scraping mud from his fingernails. "Why did she call you daughter?"

Jo squints at the road, and brushes a patch of sand from the back of her leg and turns quickly to Donnie, perhaps peeved by the question, or the intimacy of it. Donnie isn't sure.

"I'm going to tell you, it's something that nobody started intentionally. It was just something. It just cropped up. I told you my real mother passed away. Their two children are in Oregon. It was just something that we began saying. Surrogate situation, I guess."

"It's okay," Donnie says. "I'm not trying to be prying or—"

"No, it's fine," Jo says. "It's just. They're my closest friends, really. In many ways. I see them three or four times a week. So that's our ritual."

"What is?"

"What you just saw."

Donnie suddenly feels a parallel between Jo and his father's secretiveness: her attraction to shells and murk, his contained spiritual drive. Odd. Then again, she doesn't seem to have a direct agenda in life, other than keeping to herself and pursuing her interests and general welfare, and this thought passes and fizzles, and another rises: what exactly does Jo get from this old blind couple anyway? Without altruism, what is her incentive here? Obviously, this is the big question. He comes close to approaching it, yet he swerves away from it for now for some internal reason he can't put his finger on. Perhaps it's respect.

The security guards wave Jo past the gate, and she play-punches Donnie on the shoulder, and her face opens and she blinks. She tells him she'll pick him up around seven and they'll go back over to Helen and Grant's for dinner and relaxation. Donnie nods, and covers his eyes from the glare of the windshields, and he waves without looking, and inexplicably jogs to the stairwell under the shade of the overhang. Donnie stands in front of the dented maroon door, wondering how it became so marked, inhaling the thick odor of chlorine and wet sand, and he grins at the sudden and unexpected turn of this vacation, and he opens the door. He feels grounded for the first time in a long while. This will be different.

As Donnie trudges the four flights to the condo, he dreads the scrutiny he's bound to find at the breakfast table: his father criticizing his living habits, his mother pestering him with questions and insistent curiosity. He can imagine Kevin shaking his head in sympathy as he butters his bagel and trudges out to the deck to avoid getting involved. Claustrophobia isn't exactly the right word for it, but he often feels pressed-in, in need of escape.

But when Donnie unlocks the door, he walks into the condo cloaked in hushed silence. He peers around the corner of the hall awaiting something, someone. He calls out: "Mom? Dad? Kevin?" No answer. Then he realizes he still doesn't know what time it is. Damn watch. He assumes it's around 8:30, since Jo has to be at work, but he's not certain. Note to self: purchase watch. Then again, who cares? This is vacation isn't it?

Donnie walks to his bedroom, closes the door, and flops down on the bed. He feels as if he's regressing: he was just here not that long ago. Still, he feels his consciousness thinning, exhausted from the morning, from his own thoughts—as if he's experienced a whole day before he usually rises. He closes his eyes, smelling the warm plastic fragrance of the lampshade, then he flicks the light off. Donnie's eyes sting and the cool air-conditioned interior of the condo, contrary to expectations, only seem to amplify this fact. Yet, he is grateful he has the ability to have such a trivial problem, and at this his mind digresses into a memory of getting his eyes tested in middle school in a long bored line of students, and the thought of woodworking teachers who would use scare tactics to make students wear goggles. At the thought of sawdust and splinters, Donnie drifts off.

Donnie wakes up sweating. A bolt of sunlight through the skylight interrogates him, and the air-conditioning seems to have kicked off. He rises in his gummy T-shirt and peers into the kitchen to see the time (12:34), and he hears water bubbling on the stove. Mom must be in, he thinks. Then he hears voices in his parents' bedroom. He walks over to the temperature gauge and flicks the knob down, but still doesn't hear a thing. Oh well, he thinks. It should be hot anyway. Screw it.

He's just about to hustle into the shower when he hears the voices in the bedroom grow louder. He decides to go sit in the couch in the living room and play dumb. What can they say? He's not eavesdropping if they are talking this loud. The first recognizable words Donnie hears are from his mother. Her voice rises seemingly with each syllable:

"You and your personal Jesus. Is that all there is to it?"

"It's not a personal Jesus, Margaret. It's not a personal Jesus. I've told you that a thousand...how many times?"

"Who knows? Who cares?" his mother says. "Really, Gary. *Who cares?*"

"This is part of the problem then. You see things your way. I see things my way. The correct way. The only difference is I'm a professional, and you're just reading the tea leaves."

"Nice. *Nice.* That's beautiful. So now you're an elitist? Such an expert."

"It's reality. I'm part of the religion. You're *of* it."

Donnie sighs. He's heard this sort of blank theological debate over and over. His father plays high and mighty, as if he's the Pope with direct access to God. His mother gets defensive and bickers with his every interpretive point. Blah. Blah. Blah. The big question is how they got there in the first place, and why they're still together after all these years.

He picks himself up, heads for the shower.

The warm water hits him in a rush, and Donnie grabs the safety bar for stability. It must be the grogginess, but he senses something afoot, a calm before the storm, something about to change. When he was a child Donnie used to imagine he could see the future, and this is one of those times. Suddenly he can't visualize anything other than a rift, a gap, a canyon widening within him. Somehow he knows: his parents. Why didn't he think of this before?

Donnie lathers the soap in his hands, and then down his legs, across the width of his shoulders and back He thinks of the future, and what it might hold. Janet is null and void but his parents will soon fall into the fissure. And him? He will be where he has been all along, alone, wandering for a tether. Jo is just a person he met; what does he want from her anyway? A new need? A sense of guidance? Distraction? All of the above? Donnie knows this is self-interested, and wobbly at best, but the future is something. I'll have to take *some* action, he thinks. But what? He'd rather curl into some immediate nest of safety. Safety is always temporary.

Donnie turns to face the spray, and he closes his eyes. He imagines a warm rain bathing his body, dousing his head. He imagines he is in the middle of a jungle without human ties, naked and at ease, and ready to nest into a warm dry nook under a banana tree. And as he walks toward the tree and then reclines under it, pulling palm fronds over him, he senses another next to him. He knows at once from the soft milky smell: his mother opens her arms for him, and closes her eyes, and hums, and he lays his head upon her belly. He doesn't think; he does. He sinks into the fronds, and listens to the rain around him, far away from the dry shelter of the tree. He can feel his body slow. He rests and his mother hums and pats his back, and he breathes and rests, and rests, and rests.

The Janitor

1. Sunday

August lifts the bucket from beneath the storeroom sink and turns the hot water to drum the plastic bottom, squeezing soap into the rivulet. He turns the hot water higher until bubbles froth and rise to the plastic lip. Then August takes the metallic handle of the bucket, walks to the tackboard shelving behind the storeroom door and finds his favorite pair of rubber gloves—the thick orange gloves with a soft inner meshing that won't powder away onto his palm lines. He places the bucket next to the shelving, and slips on the gloves, trying to avoid touching the outside material with anything other than the plastic wrapping he tore when he opened the package. He works his fingers deep inside until only a small pocket of air separates them from the inner lining, and he pops the joints on his fingers inside as he reaches for a sponge and drops that in the soapy bucket. He rips leaf-print paper towels from the cylinder and folds them into his back pocket.

August is down the hall to the women's room. He taps, then knocks.

"Any ladies in here?" No answer. "Hello? Any ladies?"

No ladies. August pushes the door with his shoulder, careful not to jostle the water and soap in the bucket, and he's inside. He holds the door open with his foot, and withdraws the sign that reads "Cleaning in Process" from his pocket, and props it in between the door and the doorstop. He locks the inner door. When he mops the floors, he'll use the wet-floor sign that props itself on the floor, but he mopped the day before and the tiles still sheen in the fluorescence so he must have done a good job. Mopping is not every day. Mopping is once or twice a week at most.

Today he opens the first stall and lifts the horse-shoe toilet seat, squeezing the sponge in the bucket and pressing it against the far outside of the porcelain. He scrubs the outside to the narrow front part. August sloshes the sponge in the bucket and squeezes the water out, then does the other side, noticing the streaking passages and the residue of bubbles and soap. He'll return with more paper towels to dry the porcelain after he has emptied the bucket.

When August cleans the seat as well as the porcelain the seat rests on, he uses wet paper towels to swipe away the spiraled pubic hairs, and he folds the towels in half and places them on the tiled floors. Using his fingernails and callused thumb, he squeezes the sponge damp and scrubs the tacky pools of urine from the knobs where the lid connects to the base. The bowl itself is the easiest since August can use the water of the bowl to force the streaks and excrement and fragments of vomit from the surface, and dissolve the yellow stains until the white reflects the glow of the overhead fluorescence. When he finishes cleaning the toilets he pours the frothy water into the sink, and rinses the basin of the sink with water, filling the bucket with more soap and hot water for the men's room. The men's room is next.

Later August sprays the stalls and stall doors with antiseptic cleaner and uses the paper towels to dry them, depositing the used towels in the wall trash can beneath the paper towel holster, which he will empty when it fills. The men's room only offers the extra challenge of urinals, which are easily cleaned with more paper towels and cleaner. Twice a week he changes the pink sanitary dollops when he does the floors in the bathrooms. The men's room is sometimes worse, but the ladies sees more traffic and often requires far more work.

August lives down the street from the Interfaith Center, in an apartment on the bottom floor in case of fire. The Interfaith Center is an experiment—a multi-denominational building, no faith excluded. He is sixty years old.

When he was eighteen and through with high school August cleaned for a company that made the rounds among the richer New Agers and landscape painters in Santa Fe where he grew up. He saw a house consumed with fire one evening as he drove onto the street where it sat. August returned to the house the next morning to examine the remains. The right side of the house was blackened and sooty, although the left seemed unaffected. The lack of symmetry made it more jarring to him. The wide New Mexico sky makes events seem removed somehow, less connected to what initiates them. He stepped out of the company van alone, and walked towards the burnt side of the house and then stepped inside to the cinders of furniture, glass, and burnt paintings. He could see through the ceiling to the room upstairs: wires and pipes dangled from the precipice, and the room above was equally charred.

August circled to look into the upstairs hallway, but he stumbled over something and had to catch his balance. It was a statue, a bust of a man whom August had seen before, although he didn't know his name. The deep-set eyes seemed sullen and withdrawn to August, and the mouth appeared tight but powerful. He lifted the bust from the ground and into his hands and held it, taking his cotton handkerchief from his pocket and wiping the soot and ashes from the face of the bust; it had survived. Carrying the bust to the company van, he wedged it under the passenger seat where it would be safe.

Sitting in the nursery school room in the Interfaith Center, August eats his lunch at the small table. He sits on the floor with the kiddy chairs around him. The table is made of tack board, covered with a plastic sheen, and the sun daubs the table through the humid summer air and hits the stained rug and paper bag August wrinkles open: potato bread with margarine and a piece of fruit. He tastes the heavy bread in his mouth and the film of margarine against the roof of his mouth. The dust motes float in the rectangles of sun. The aqua blue paint seems thicker and still fresh. Alphabet posters on the south wall brighten in the light; they must fade and be replaced in time by more nursery school teachers and aids that come and go each year.

August has worked at the Interfaith Center since he was twenty-five, when he ran over a girl by accident and had to stop driving. Walking is enough, just fine. When he leaves the Center he will stroll home, following the sidewalk and the paths that run through Columbia until he reaches his apartment ten minutes away. The paths lead him there. Everything is within reach. Most everyday things are easily enough acquired.

Outside he can hear the whisking of cars in the sunlight, but the playground fence blocks the view. The air conditioner clicks. The temperature is good. Room four needs attending to, and then he can go. Peeling the banana. Unfolding the paper the boss gave him. Checking to make sure: Stack five and six. Trash. Toilets. Change bulbs in the corridor to room four. Sweep foyer. Polish corridors. All these tasks are completed, and August scratches "toilets" with a single line that digs into the paper with the ballpoint and tears it through "ets."

When boredom arrives, August pictures the bust. He keeps it next to the television, on a table by the window overlooking the apartment complex lawn. During the summer, the apartment complex hires workers to cut the grass, and sometimes the whirring mower blades wake him at sunrise. He'll sit up from the carpet and walk to the bathroom and splash his face, and think of the Interfaith Center air conditioner, and how he could buy one if he wanted to. But then what? How would that change his life in any way, or improve it? Being hot isn't the end of the world. He can suffer.

Awake, the bust will seem solid and robust on the table in the coolness of the morning, and August will walk to it and unsheathe it, letting the towel slump to the side of it. The face is deep with wrinkles and seems friendly through the sadness, seemingly wise. A powerful certainty lies behind his pinched stare. Confidence. As if just a link of experiences and thoughts lie behind the eyes, which seem distilled for one moment before a shower.

He stacks the unneeded chairs and uses the dolly to move them to the side wall nooked by the indented sound-reduction bricks. Hard plastic chairs. Brown and gray with metal links so the chairs can stay in rows. New chairs arrived last year, wooden with pink and gray upholstery, but only for room one. These chairs are old as the building and as August's stint at the Interfaith Center. Most have bubble gum stuck under the seat, and August knows where to put his hands, and where not to. The children come and go. The services begin and end, and priests and pastors and rabbis enter and leave, some nodding to August, some ignoring him, some wishing him luck and grace on Sundays. August can hear the empty clatter of the hard plastic against itself in the room, large enough to seat a thousand. He can hear the reverberations of his own grunts when he pries the dolly wheels into motion.

When he finishes, August double checks the kitchen for roaches, and checks the faucets. The sun is lower in the afternoon as he walks towards the offices to check the doors. Saturdays are not nearly as busy, and only one service is active in room one until three thirty. He can hear a preacher exhorting far off down the corridor. And another voice. These are calming sounds.

"Hey, Duke." It's Ray, who has come to work the night until twelve. He's wearing slacks with a plaid shirt and his glasses glitter in a field of sun he's walking from. August shields his eyes from the glare. He likes 'Duke,' however he earned the nickname.

"What's wrong?" Ray's carrying a blue hand-cooler in one hand and a radio in the other. August shields his eyes from the sun glint.

"I can't see you, man."

"Summmmmmmertime," Ray croons.

"You got that right." Ray places his radio on the floor, and the two friends shake hands.

"Hey, watch where you're putting that," August jokes. "I just did all the dirty work."

"I'm telling you." Ray points around the foyer and then tilts his head to say 'job well done.' "This place shines." The preacher's voice rises and falls. Ray's shoes squeak on the floor. "Hey, have you met the kid?"

"Who?"

"Zachary's son," Ray says. "You know, the kid. The kid." Zachary is the building manager.

"I didn't know. When did Zachary get a son?" Ray's pupils dilate, and he turns to an invisible audience behind him laughing. August thumbs a shirt button.

"I don't know, man. Jesus, where have you been? He's a good kid. He's young."

"Zachary isn't too old himself."

"That's right. Hey, anything from him today?"

"No."

"Okay then," Ray says. "See you."

"See you then."

Once when August stepped out of his shower onto the red crumpled towel he used as a bath mat, he reached for the lamp above the cabinet mirror and shocked himself turning it on. It felt as if a grizzly grabbed him from behind, and he jumped. He doesn't tell Ray these small details. There is sensitivity and trust, but not as much as he'd like sometimes.

The next day August sits on a bench on the wooded path behind his apartment. He thinks of the man in New Mexico who watched his aspens for wasps, using binoculars, climbing his aspens with a ladder to inspect for damage despite hurting his back. The man walked up and down his street checking the other cars for speeding. The man was once a truck driver, he said. But he couldn't do that any longer.

When August sits in the woods, he feels as if he understands the despondency of people. When he swept the floor of the Interfaith Center with the push broom, collecting the dust at the far ends of the corridors, he watches the joggers circle the track at the high school across the parking lot, white sneakers glowing in the darkening sky. So many thoughts. Different brains churning around the same thoughts, thoughts not unlike his own thoughts, August knows. But that feeling only lasts for a second, and then it's gone.

August walks through the afternoon heat, watching the sidewalk grill in the heat. On his days off he swims at the indoor pool, treads water until he warms, does the backstroke in the pool lanes and views the ladies. Tonight, he decides he will not listen to the game on the fuzzy transformer, or think about living within his own skin. Entertaining others, making others feel less sorry for themselves. These things meant something to him. Yet August knows he lacked the energy or resourcefulness to make it work.

He decides to eat at the café, although he gave up hamburgers a few years ago along with cigarettes and alcohol. Now he buys a chicken salad sandwich and a soda and rests in front of the television afterwards. Filling your time is one of the most difficult...Just finding things to do. Sometimes, August plays chess with himself, walk to the Wilde Lake Village Center and observes the children play on the playground, as they hold the hands of their mothers and swing on them. Anything but direct confrontational loneliness...even more work, something to distract him. Something to watch, to view.

When Ray takes over, sometimes August stays and helps, just for the distraction. He couldn't afford to buy a movie ticket often. Once a month maybe he'd go to the movies, and that would fill time. The most difficult stretch is when work ends and the rest of the night is his only.

The restaurant has an outdoor seating area and August orders his sandwich and soda and sits at a white plastic table with a pink carnation and stares at the carnation. The stem seems so green and alive, and the way it sits speared in the water soaking it up seems new to August, although he had seen it many times. The splayed leaves are so perfect they look plastic, but they aren't, and maybe the veneer of the table affects the way he sees it. The café is almost empty. A couple sits on the other side of the outdoor café, looking off in different directions, drinking their sodas. The man leans back in his chair and sips from a plastic straw. The woman pulls her hair back from her face and glances up at the man and pops the lid from her drink. Soda wells from her mouth and fizzes onto the table and she forces a pained smile, but the man eyes a couple walking, each holding one hand of a child.

The high school kids lathered the chicken salad sandwich with too much mayonnaise, and the rye bread is overly soggy. August shakes his head and takes the plastic plate with the sandwich, and unfolds a napkin on top of it and walks toward the lake.

August likes the fact that James Rouse, who designed the planned community of Columbia, himself lived on the lake. Once they met. Rouse was in the Interfaith Center for a ceremony. The other people dressed in nice clothes—dresses and ties and slacks and high-heeled shoes. Rouse asked him where the bathroom was, and August told him. Rouse smiled and thanked August, and then asked him if he had been working at the Interfaith Center long. August told him, and Rouse said that he thought August was doing a good job. Later August noticed that his fly was partially down. He promptly zipped it up, aghast at his negligence. Rouse died a couple years ago and though August did not attend the funeral he mourned quietly, in his own way.

August sits on the edge of the pier with the plastic plate and chicken salad sandwich, and he plucks clumps of bread from the sandwich and tosses them into the water. The mallards squawk after them, and dunk into the water. August enjoys these little things, listening to the game on the radio, fishing at the lake, swimming, feeding the ducks at the lake, sitting on a log on the paths of Columbia. If he had more money he would buy a house on the lake so he could wake up in the morning and touch his bust, and look over the lake and fish and swim in the lake at once, and he would be content as any person. Someday he would like to be soothed by water. Picking the bread, he looks over his shoulder at his own arm. The odd angle makes it seem deformed.

At home he toasts more potato bread, and spreads margarine on the burnt outer crust, and eats it with orange juice. Television is good for these moments, he thinks. He watches a game show with the sound turned low. The wheel turns, the ball bounces. People clap and smile, and then the screen jumps to ads.

Later Zachary calls in August's cushiony half-sleep.

"Hi, August."

"Hello, Mr. Tulane. How are you?"

"Good, good." His boss is a kind man with a voice that tries to smooth things over, not too hard, earnest. "Let me tell you what's on the slate for tomorrow. Okay, my son is going to be working with you. He's fourteen. I should have told you earlier, I apologize."

"Very good," August says.

"It's his first job, August. He needs extra cash so he can save for a car when he gets old enough. That's just down the road now."

"That's nice."

"He's a hard worker and I think you'll get along fine," Zachary says.

"Okay."

"So I'll bring him by after school ends for him. Around three thirty, after you get there tomorrow. Is that okay with you? Can you help him get acclimated?"

"That's fine." 'Help' means down the road to the end, winding down flaccid and groping for something else to hang onto. Baby-sitting.

"I think you'll get along fine. He plays baseball. Maybe you can talk about baseball with my son. I think he'll be a good helper for you."

"Okay," August says.

"Okay, well...I think I'll see you tomorrow then."

"Okay. What's his name?"

"Ryan. His name is Ryan."

"Ryan, huh."

"Yup, Ryan. I'll pick him up around 9:00 so he can get to bed early enough. It is a school night."

2. Monday

The goal isn't to clean every nook and cranny, August knows, but to do what's asked, fulfill work routines, then relax or try to relax when all is done. Then you are a rudimentary security guard; then you just make sure everything is safe. At three the sun is too strong for window washing, and the offices are still in use. So he decides to steam clean in room number three: hot water extraction. August mixes the chemicals and water, and places the container in the cleaner. This is necessary only twice a year—the monthly dry powder cleaning just spreads it around the already dirty carpet. It is good to take care of things in the building, to care for it.

He plugs the machine into the closest outlet. He has already cleared the room, except for the piano. This he will move later, roll it out of the way when he gets to that corner. August moves the machine into the far end of the room. He will cut the room by going along the edges. He has already put carpet protectors under the furniture legs to prevent rust stains. He will overlap his strokes, working his way toward the center of the room, careful not to douse the carpet too heavily with water. Too much will ruin the backing, too little won't thoroughly clean the carpeting.

When August holds down the trigger, the water sprays and the machine froths into motion. He trudges up the room through the fluorescence and chemical smells, and he pivots and turns back on the far side of the room. In his head he whistles a song from way back. This is the easy part. This isn't bonnet cleaning with multiple tasks and components. Shampooing the carpet is simply done; it's moving the furniture that gives August difficulties. When Ryan comes in he'll help with the piano. Then August will use a grooming brush to straighten the fibers, and he will use fans to dry the area so people can do whatever they need to do.

The bases would be loaded if he walked this guy. Men on second and third, two outs. 3-3 in the top of the ninth, 2 and 2 count. September and crisp; he leaned over for the sign. He nodded at the fastball. Big slugger up, and the crowd was on him. What has happened to him? What happened to his stuff? Yeah, once he was the young firebrand rookie with a heater in the high 90's and a snapping curve ball, a full change. But why was he the one out there now in this crucial game? Common opinion: he was burnt. He partied too much. He drank too much, snorted too much coke. His arm weighed down in all that sin and substance. In 1966 August was 24 years old, but he felt fifty.

The guy on third seemed to be mocking him, that little smirky wink. August watched the guy on second take a large lead, directly in front of short. His confidence was so low he felt he might throw the ball away if he tried a pickoff. The runner on third might bolt for home, and that would be it. He had to be careful.

The crowd was on their feet. And the guy danced back and forth, hot-dogging. He said "throw the ball, pansy." August snapped the ball to third, and the guy dove back. August walked off the mound towards third, caught the throw back. August wiped the sweat off his brow. He was perspiring heavily. Brown, dirty sweat all over his arms and face.

"What did you say to me?" August kept walking towards him.

"Get back on the mound, asshole," the third baseman said. The runner smirked more widely.

"Fuck that," August said, walking right up to the runner at third. "I said, what did you say to me?"

"Don't know what you're talking about," the runner said, cackling. The third baseman pushed August away. The third base umpire was suddenly there. "Okay, ladies, let's finish this game sometime today."

August yelled and pointed at the runner. August eyed him, eyed the man on second. The pitching coach was running toward the mound. Told him he better straighten himself up. They need this game, he said, and even more than that the team needs the old August back, that firebrand. The pitching coach told him he's got to cut the parties, the womanizing, get his head together. "Come on man, one fastball and we're up, chance to win. Let's get this done."

August was back on the rubber, head all over the place. Sweat soaking through his shirt, down his back into his pants. He took his hat off, and wiped the sweat, put it back on, even wetter than before. It wasn't hot; nobody else seemed to be sweating. August bent over and the sweat dripped onto his shoes, onto the dirt. The catcher flashed the signs again. Fastball still. Upright, ready to pitch, August glanced back at second, thought about throwing—too risky—still didn't feel ready to pitch the ball. He glared at the guy at third who was making kissing faces at August. He quick-tossed the ball over again, and the runner dove back on the far side of the bag and snuck his hand in before the tag.

The crowd was restless. The crowd could always tell when something's not right. "Pitch the ball," some guy yelled from behind the plate. "Come on August," a lady yelled. "*Pitch the ball,*" another guy shouted from above the visitor's dugout. He leaned over the rubber again. The runner on third took another large lead. The runner on second was well off the bag.

The catcher lifted his mitt. The slugger waved his bat slowly behind his head. August considered all the options, and decided on the one nobody expected: he whirled around and threw towards second. But the pick-off play caught the shortstop off guard: he couldn't get to the ball. The baseball sailed over second into center field. The crowd sucked its breath. The runner on third walked home. The runner on second, motored around third, headed for home. The throw came in right, but too late. August was pulled and the Orioles lost the game 5-3. That night there was no comeback.

August remembers one night in particular, the year before. He was at the Kat Club on 86th Street. New York was the kind of place he liked because you didn't have to go looking for trouble. He was with his roommate and party pal Nils Dugan, and they had four women with them, hanging all over them. They were professional athletes, and they could do what they wanted. They didn't care who the women were or where they were from or really anything about them. They didn't have to. In the crowded nightclub August popped a baggy out, and cut some lines on a flip-up mirror in his palm. The six of them huddled over his palm, and did lines right there. If anybody noticed, they didn't say anything.

They ordered whisky sours and Manhattans for the ladies and drank three or four, dancing until they could feel the rush pour all over them. And they called a cab. "Go to our hotel, wherever it is," August said. "Hey, screw all you ladies!" Nils would straighten it out. He was married. August had his hand up the skirt of one, while the other one was on his lap with her shirt off, rubbing up and down his chest. Baseball groupies were easily found. They did more lines, and slunk into the belly of the hotel.

Everything was fine until two of the husbands showed up, and beat the players. First they used their fists, then they used bats. Then the husbands sat on the players' torsos and pummeled their faces while the women watched terrified. Three of the women ran out into the hall, half naked and crying, coked and drunk out of their minds. Then they started laughing. The other woman watched, biting her fingernails, and swaying her head back and forth. August remembers the slam of the hotel door, the bawling. He remembers the woman who was still there laughing at his mangled face.

"Don't cry, little pansy," she said. "You are a major league player!"

"I'm not a baby," August said. "I'm a professional—" He looked around. Blood on the rug. Nils was passed out. For a second August thought Nils might be dead. He shook his body, telling him to wake up, wake up, wake up. He did, and then he passed out again.

And then there was the time when he was sent down. End of 1966, three weeks after the game against the Yankees. A few weeks before the series August was sent down. The former Rookie of the Year, three years later—nothing. He wouldn't see the limelight again. Coach asked him to come into his office like he had many times, trying to straighten him out, trying to make it work. But the kid's E.R.A. was 6.47, the highest on the team, one of the highest in the A.L. The press caught wind of his doings. The fans hated him. His teammates thought he was a cocky prick. Coach said he thought morale was lower than it should have been considering they were in first place by a mile. He told August to sit down. The bright blue office smelled of fresh paint, fumy.

"Why didn't they paint this office orange, coach?"

"You mean team colors?"

"Yeah, I thought they would paint it the team colors," August said. "You ever looked at orange, son?"

"No," August said.

"It's butt-ugly. It's bright, and it hurts your eyes. I asked them please, please, please paint it something I can be comfortable with. Something cool. Something relaxing. I like being comfortable."

"Me too, coach."

"You do?"

"I think I do. I mean, I like having things I want to have, that kind of thing."

"That's not what I mean, son."

"What do you mean?" August asked.

"To me 'comfortable' means I don't have to try to force a square peg into a round hole. Get my deal? I don't have to force anything anywhere. My view is this: I don't want to make something out of something that is not meant to be."

"I see." August was numb, as if it had already happened and he was witnessing it over and over.

"You believe in fate or any of that other bullshit?"

"I guess so."

"Yeah, I guess I do too. Here's the situation, son."

"Go ahead, coach."

"I do feel horrible about it, but it is my decision. I don't want to bullshit with you about that. I'm the bad guy. I'm the one you can hate when you're trying to get back. Somehow things got messy with you. Either you're the square peg or I am, or the team is. It doesn't really matter. Something gives."

"Yeah," August said.

"Yeah?"

"I know what you're—"

"Good, good, that's going to make it easier if you can see yourself—"

"Right," August said. Part of him knew that was it; he would never get back.

"What matters is one of us is the round hole. One of them has to go because. You know the because."

"Yeah," August says. "I got the because."

Ryan arrives at the right moment. August is finished with the shampooing and he has wheeled the machine out into the hallway. He has emptied the container twice, and he's dumping the third, full of chemicals and dirt accumulated from Sunday receptions, day care, and Circle K meetings. In the storeroom he raps the container against the sink and rinses it out. He watches the bubbles in the water as they flush the grunge down the drain hole. He finds the grooming brush and walks back to the room to tend to the fibers.

As he's walking down the hall, he sees a boy in a light blue windbreaker and black jeans, paint splattered boots that look like they belong to his father. August slows. Under the windbreaker he can see the top scrawl of the Orioles logo. A rectangle sits in the boy's windbreaker pocket. The boy wears a baseball cap, pulled backwards and he is looking the other direction, tapping his foot against the tile nervously. He has one hand in his jeans pocket. He takes the hand out and begins thrumming it against his thigh to some invisible music in his head. The boy bobs his head along with his hand. His hand jingles some change in his pocket and then nuzzles back into the pocket, and he turns around. His dinner is in a paper bag in his other hand.

August watches what the boy's reaction. The boy has probably heard about August, but doesn't have a picture in his head. And now it's all picture, and what will he do with it? What will this relationship be like? Who exactly is this person and what will he ask of me? Will I even be affected by this in the long run, and how much more do I care than I am pretending not to. Why does this moment seem important, even if it's not?

August walks slowly towards the boy, and the boy takes his hand out of his pocket. The wind pops against the glass. August can smell the fetid wetness of the ferns and spider plants, which he just watered. A long Buick drives by and speeds up around the corner of the parking lot. The sun has retreated enough, and the light is softened; they can wash windows. August pushes his arm through the brownish light and shakes the boy's hand.

"Hi, I'm August. Pleasure to meet you, really!"

"My name's Ryan."

"Good to meet you, man."

"Yeah, uh-huh."

August walks Ryan through the building. The tour is languorous enough that Ryan will have the chance to take to him, and expect to work—but not too hard—expect to have a little fun along the way. The kid's hard to read though. August can't tell if he's really there, or if he really wants to be there. Or if his father is making him come, for some other unstated purpose. He shows the kid all the big service rooms, and the smaller meeting rooms, the nursery rooms, the bathrooms, the offices where Ryan's father works. He makes a big deal out of that. Hopefully the kid gets along with his father. He shows the kid the baptismal, and the nursery school playground. The kid clinks his change, yawns. "Okay, whatever," Ryan says. "Now what?"

"*Now* what?" August repeats. "I was thinking wash the windows. That might be a good first job for you."

"Sounds fine with me, man."

August doesn't like how he calls him "man." There is something bigheaded about that.

In the storeroom August finds the thin rectangular bucket to hold the squeegees, and he finds the brass squeegees themselves. He checks the sponges to make sure they aren't ripped, and he makes sure the connections are tight to the t-shaped handles.

"This is what we will use to wash the windows," August says. "I'll show you what we need to do. It is simple." August waves the kid over to the sink. He places the bucket in the sink basin. "This is the most important room for this job, and we should have everything we need here." August walks back over to the shelving, but the kid doesn't follow him. The shelving holds the cleaning materials, August says. He finds the ammonia, and the alcohol. The copper measuring spoons are hanging from the faucet. A teaspoon of alcohol is all you need. Ammonia until it smells strong enough so that you have to wear a mouth cover. The water fills the bucket. August asks the kid if he could fetch two masks from the door. They quiver on the rack of hooks on the back of the door. The kid doesn't move.

"What for? I don't need one of them or anything."

"Yes you do, son. I'm telling you, you'll need it when the fumes get strong enough."

"I don't think that's going to happen." August thinks, it's his decision. The kid has to come to his own realizations, as we all do. But he'd rather the kid just listen to his advice.

"You do whatever you want. I'm telling you what I think would be best."

"Whatever. Let's just do it," Ryan says.

The kid still doesn't move from the sink. He leans against the sink basin, and puts his hand in his pocket. He starts tapping his foot. The kid is trying not to appear bothered, but he's too attentive to August to be truly apathetic. If he really didn't care, his eyes would glaze over. Ryan's eyes are wide open.

"Could you please get me my mask then?"

"Get your own mask, man," Ryan says. August watches the kid. The kid has both hands in his pockets now, paper bag sticking out of one pocket; the hands are in clods in his pocket; the toes in his boots are knotting and unknotting. This kid is in some unknown territory. August will give him a break. Get to business. Smooth over any rough elements himself. Then matters will be easier down the road, which counts more than a signature battle. August walks over to the door and takes the mask, snaps it over his face, and trudges back to the sink basin and turns the water off. He stirs the solution with a paint stick. He pats Ryan on the shoulder, and Ryan doesn't recoil. He doesn't move a muscle.

"You will learn, son," August says. "No more, 'man.'"

They go right out front, to the sixteen-foot windows. August says he wants to start there while the sun still gives them enough natural light. They should be able to finish, he says, before the sun goes down. The clatter of computers and the whooshing copy machine sounds open into the hallway when the office door swings, and someone claps down the hall in the direction of their car out front. It's Reverend Williams, and August waves to him. The Reverend smiles and says he hopes that August has a nice evening. August says he's going to try to, and say hello to your wife for me. Ryan sags his head, and winces. August knows what that's for, but he's not going to mention it. Ryan digs the two squeegees into the grouting between the tiles. Two chamois cloths rest in August's back pocket. That should be enough.

August takes one of the squeegees from Ryan and dips it into the bucket. He will turn to his right and tell Ryan that this is the way it is done. First apply the solution with the strip washer, but don't drip it on the floor. Get it wet enough that the entire pane is covered. Now take the squeegee side and go along the top edge of the windowpane, at a slight angle, just slight. Dry the blade quickly with the chamois so it doesn't streak. Go again along the next strip. Do it again. Do it again. Dot it again. With the cloth wipe the dirty water off the sill without touching the glass. Touch up any missed spots or streaks. Go on to the next window. This is the easiest way, August explains. This is the way I learned.

"Now it's your turn," August says. "We'll share the

bucket." The kid grinds his teeth together and reaches back for his baseball cap for assurance. He pulls it one eighty to block out the sun, and spears his strip washer into the bucket. The water sloshes from side to side, but not enough to rise over the lip.

"Be careful now," August says.

"Yeah whatever." The office door swings open again, and a man and a woman stop, and talk behind the partition that separates the foyer from the office hallway. The man says that he can't understand why Zachary is doing this and that, but that he doesn't think it's smart strategically. The woman says she just doesn't think it's shrewd one way or another. Zachary is ineffectual; Zachary is too *nice*; Zachary isn't the boss he could be.

"We don't want to alienate the Baptists," the man says. "That's the risk he's really taking with this."

"And this is supposed to be *non-denominational*," the woman says. "Of course, I'm not. But he has to be. I don't know, the decision seems a bit strong to me. Not harsh, but definitely strong." Ryan pretends not to care, pretends not to hear, this time to his advantage. Or perhaps he doesn't really care one way or another what other people think of his father, or maybe he would agree with them. The strip washer hits the glass and water squeezes off, too fast, too fast, down to the sill. Ryan looks slightly shocked at how much comes out.

"Move it around some," August says. "It's okay. Just move it around. Spread it."

August thinks about taking the washer in his hands and showing him what he means, but he decides he'll just let Ryan try, and not that much can go wrong anyway. This element of showing someone the ropes is the hardest: just let them fall or fly on their own, let them make their own self-adjustments. August has to have enough faith in Ryan to let him go. And he does; Ryan spreads the water all around.

The man lowers his voice so that August can't hear them anymore, and he wonders if they heard a noise and realized they were in the company of others, or if they crept down the hall, or went back into the office. But if they went back into the office August would have heard the rush of clattering and talking. August doesn't hear anything.

"Good, Ryan. Fine." Ryan finishes wetting the window and turns to August.

"Now I wipe it off?"

"That's right. Just make sure you press hard enough so you're taking the water off." Ryan places it against the window. "Get it all the way to the edge, so it can't dribble down the side." Ryan presses it flush.

"Good, good," August says. "Good." August pats him on the shoulder, on the back.

Later, after the staff clears out, August shows Ryan how to clean the rooms in the office suite. You take two large trash bags for trash and a handful of small replacement trash bags to put in the small cans. Take the vacuum cleaner too. And since there is two of them tonight, August says, one can do one job and one can do the other. Ryan says he'll vacuum, fine. August hustles from office cranny to lockable office door, lugging the trash bags that are full enough or messy enough, throwing them into the larger bag. He leaves the small bags that are empty or that just have a few wrappers or pieces of paper, picking the refuse out of them with the very tips of his fingers.

And Ryan vacuums each area, and each room, after August takes care of the trash, always after August says. It's important not to rustle anything in the offices, or alter the look of anything. No disruptions. The idea, August says, is to be in and out as quickly and invisibly as possible. You want to disappear. You want your lack of presence to be felt. If anyone thinks you were there, it's usually because something is not right: bits of shredded paper still on the carpet, dust on the windowsill. A good janitor is in the background, the best place to be. You disappear.

After this, August shows Ryan the checklist that Zachary made. Ryan says he doesn't want to eat until later. They do need to vacuum all the rooms, or at least pick up the visible trash. There are no services on Tuesdays, so those rooms don't need set up. They should clean out the refrigerator and oven in the kitchen, but that is not top priority. Then they just need to *be there* to make sure nobody suspicious comes in, make sure to lock up by ten. Two months ago a vandal scrawled "KKK" on the bathroom wall. August was in the office area, cleaning out, and he left the doors unlocked, as he usually does. Who would vandalize a center of worship? He called the police. No arrest was made, at least so far.

August and Ryan do vacuum all the rooms, and they do clean the kitchen, and by that time it is 8:30 p.m. Ryan's father is coming at 9:00. August finds his small transformer radio. They sit in room three, the huge service room, and August turns on the Orioles game. The Orioles are losing three-one, in the third.

"You like baseball?" Ryan asks him. His cap is on

backwards again. He still jingles his change, but his foot has stopped tapping.

"I think baseball is…a great game," August says. He leans back in his chair and closes his eyes. "It's the best game there is."

"You really think that?"

"Yeah, I do."

They sit and listen to the game together as the Orioles go down in order, and the Blue Jays come up to bat and push one across with a solo shot. Then television ads. And the Orioles don't score again, and then more ads, and the Blue Jays score another one on two back-to-back doubles. The fans in Toronto are rowdy. Ryan pulls the rectangle out of his windbreaker. August thinks cigarettes. He thinks he's going to light up, or try to right there. But it's some kind of hard candy. Ryan pops a yellow one into his mouth.

"Here, you want one?" He holds a red one out to August. August shakes his head.

"Got to watch my sugar intake these days," he says.

"Yeah, I know. I stopped drinking sodas."

"Good for you, Ryan."

They listen to another inning, as the Orioles push one across with a double, a grounder to the right side, a long sac fly.

"I don't know," Ryan says. "Everybody like says the Cubs and Red Sox are the big chokers. It might be the Orioles though."

"Could be," August says. "You're probably right."

"Every year they find a way to disappoint."

"Hey, Ryan."

"Yeah?"

"Don't let those other people in the office bother you when you're here."

"What do you mean?"

"Don't be embarrassed," August says. "Don't worry what other people think."

"I'm not embarrassed."

"All right, just don't be. Nothing to be ashamed of."

"I know. You don't have to tell me."

Even over the game they can both hear Zachary's Toyota beeping at the curb.

"He doesn't want to come in?" Ryan says.

"Doesn't look that way."

Ryan reaches out his hand for August and they shake.

"See you next time," Ryan says.

3. Tuesday

If he walks up the path, in the opposite direction from the Village Center, August can reach the swimming pool in the blocky building with glass windows painted white. On his days off, this is part of his circuit. He tries to arrive as early as possible, when the professional ladies are pulling into their parking spaces, quickly striding into the locker room, changing, diving into the pool to do their laps before they have to rush off to work. August likes the feeling of hurried procession, women on the verge. He changes into his bathing suit and pretends to limber along the side, watching the ladies. Just watching. Is there anything wrong with just watching?

Today there are the two friends in the same lane, a

bouncy woman with reddish hair, and a taller trim woman with a white swimming cap. He's seen them before. A debonair woman in her fifties enters, folds her plush towel over the back of a pool chair, takes her glasses off, and places them on the seat, snaps her own swimming cap over her head and chooses the lane to the far right. She catches August's eye and snaps her head back to the water, not wanting to know where his glance falls, or pretending not to. She sits on the ledge and shudders instinctively at the cool water, then slips into the water, holding her arms rigid against her body. She ducks into the pool and starts on a slow, bobbing breaststroke. August bends over and touches his toes, reaches back and grabs his foot. Chlorine, gentle splashes, and exhales. Water vapor.

Two ladies depart talking together, heads leaning inward. One is a younger woman—doe faced, pouty lips, brown hair in a bob, beautiful wrists and bikini. The other is plain with a sly mouth, thin lips, thick ankles, a big poof of hair, darker—Latina or Greek?—dressed in a full-length black suit. Bikini woman is laughing in quick got-one-over-on-you bursts.

"Now *that's* a man for you," she says.

"Well, well. I think I'd just say 'Looky what we have here,' and the rest would be old history."

"Tillie!"

"You know what I mean," the plain one says. "So what will you do next time?"

"Well, I'm not going to charge him with harassment, because I have to admit—"

"There's still that attitude like, 'come on don't be so'—"

"'So, so, *serious*.' We don't want to be seriousssss," bikini says. The plain one nods in agreement, and they both laugh.

They toss their towels onto a single chair, and choose the lane next to the other women that all know each other. They are among friends. Morning ritual friends.

The pool is divided into the solitary and the sisterly. August won't approach anyone, but there is nothing wrong with watching, is there? He felt pangs of guilt the first few times, but this is a public pool isn't it? This is a place where he should be able to just exist. To breathe and take it all in. It's not his fault if most of the swimmers are women. The older woman kicks up a spray of water and August watches it curl out and hang in the air, glob and blop in mid-air, then fall slowly back into the water from where it came.

And then another man walks out, a short, balding man with sunburn, some executive type trying to ward off heart disease or love handles. And the trance is over for August. He stands up straight as he can and walks along the edge of the pool, not looking up at the other man, or the women doing laps. He can hear the classy woman breathing rhythmically, exhale, stroke, stroke, stroke and exhale. He chooses a lane in the middle, and jumps in with a splash he hopes they all feel, and he starts into a slow freestyle stroke.

August's sister, Claire, lives five minutes away, past the pool in a townhouse cluster. She called last week, said he should come over on one of his off days. Her husband works for the Defense Department in Washington, and she's alone most of the day. Never wanted to work herself; she's the social planner of August's family. Vick, their brother, should also be at Claire's today; they are all close, the three of them. Tuesday is the regular day. Vick's a cabby, off most mornings. August decides he'll swing by, and she'll have breakfast for him, or at least coffee.

He loves walking these paths. The sensory experience: the smell of the oaks, the clackering birds, the asphalt, smell of dirt, dust, pine needles, moss, grass. Growing up in New Mexico was a different experience. The whole counted for more, but the small things in life passed him by. Sometimes August thinks that's what contributed to his problems on the field. It wasn't the drugs, the alcohol, the women; it was his lack of attention. He couldn't concentrate, couldn't exist one minute to the next. He wasn't thinking with the right part of his brain.

Does he wish he married? No. Yes. Maybe? How could he after his complete collapse? Then the accident: he was a bull in a china closet; how could a man like that offer anything to anyone for any period of time? But he was lonely, seared with a loneliness that seems to scorch a red line right through him. He walks around these paths feeling marked. The trees loom over him, not in any impressionistic or foreboding way. They are just trees. But, August wonders, are these trees taller today? Does the sky cast a blanket over him in the same way? Do other people feel so small and humbled by these things?

There was a woman a few years ago, Wendy, who worked part time for the Slayton House at the Village Center, answering phones, arranging the art work in the gallery and overseeing the building activities. She would drop by the Interfaith Center after work and bring August a sandwich from the café, or a soda, or a bag of pretzels, although August would only eat a few. August would visit her at the Slayton house. She would cook him dinner at her apartment, pick him up in her car since she lived fifteen minutes away and off the bus line. If he loved any woman in his life, he loved Wendy. Two years of his life were filled with a level of happiness that was greater than any other he had experienced up to that point. She would bring dinner to his apartment, mother him like a child.

And the apartment smelled like yams topped with butter and pepper and sea salt. Trout with lemon spray, homemade fresh bread, dry white wine. She brought a touch of class and beauty into his life. He decided to tell her the real reason his baseball career died. He told her before that he had an arm injury, and she felt bad for him, but how much of their closeness was based on pity? Maybe she benefited from living in his afterglow? What would she make of him if he explained his life? He couldn't *not* tell her any more. She was too good to him—for reasons he didn't entirely comprehend.

They ate, smiling at each other as usual. They conversed about other jobs they held at one time or another. They both agreed that they would rather not work a job that would sap their energy; they wanted a job that they could do in their sleep. Their lives were somewhere outside on the edge of what most people considered "respectable" perhaps. But their lives were also the walks in the park, the canoeing and the dinners together. Exertion was peripheral. Wendy admired August for this, and she shared his outlook. She said he was unusually self-conscious about this. August looked at this human being and blinked.

"Why do you *care* about me at all?"

"Are you kidding? You're a good man," she said. "A very good man."

"There are many good men. Spending time with me can't exactly be that exciting."

"Who needs exciting? I didn't ask you to entertain me. This is life."

Wendy was forty-two at the time, divorced. She wore a ski sweater, with a white, and purplish-black fringe around the neck. A pink dress shirt slapped out of the sweater hole. She still wore her wedding ring. Her brown hair was fringed with gray. She wore copper hoop earrings, curled at the far end of the circle. Her hands were warm and veiny, and she never stooped to makeup, or fingernail polish.

After dinner she would sit on the floor and rest her head on his leg. She often seemed too fine and beautiful for sex. He didn't want to spoil anything. He would sip wine, and she would tell him stories about her past, her family. Her hopes. Her desires. This time she groaned contentedly.

"I have something that you might like."

"Okay, shoot."

"You know, I told you about my past, about my baseball…"

"Yes, of course. A bit."

"Well, there is something I need to tell you about that," he said. She propped her head on his leg with her chin, blew her hair out of her face. Her breath smelled like the best parts of dinner. She blinked.

"What's that?"

"It wasn't because I threw out my arm. I was an asshole."

"What happened?"

"What happened? I drank too much and did drugs and screwed as many women as I could. That was my mistake. 'Success' and all that. I was an idiot." As August expected there was a long silence. Yet he didn't feel any tension from her; it was all self-motivated. He needed to tell her so he could feel he was being truthful. Maybe that was foolish. Who knows the real truth about anyone anyway? It was redundant. She patted him on the thigh, and put her head back on his leg.

"Don't you want to say anything?"

"I'm sorry to hear you think you made mistakes. It doesn't really matter though, you know. I'm not here judging you. That is the *past*." But August was judging himself. He hadn't addressed the basic elements of his life and he felt uncomfortable with his own self-assessment. Shame, bitterness, self-loathing. The past was the past, but it was still part of who he *was*. He couldn't abolish his memory or the consequences. He couldn't repeatedly face someone he respected. A month later he told her he'd rather be alone.

It would be easier for him to just be alone.

Knock, knock. "There he is," Vick says. It suddenly feels colder to August. The wind picks up and seems wet and heavy. "I told you he'd come today. I could *feel* it."

Vick opens the door, wearing a black turtleneck and jeans. He sticks both his hands out, shakes August's right between them. August carries his swimming gear in a plastic bag in the other hand.

"Hey, brother," he says. "How's everything?"

"Everything's everything."

"Come on in, we're just starting breakfast. Drop your bag there, I guess." He waves to the side table. Next to the phone.

Claire's kitchen is compact and orderly. The cupboards

are primly kept, nothing stacked on top. The refrigerator is clean outside and inside. The walls are decorated in a country style, painted wood hearts, little animals, lace-embroidered plaques, country signs. A small oval pine table sits in the corner. Vick pulls a chair out for August, tells him to sit down. He nods, but Claire's already giving him a hug in front of the stove. She pats him on the back and gives him a peck on the ear.

Then August sits down. Claire serves both of them scrambled eggs, English muffins and coffee. Utensils are on the table. The cream is in a little cow pitcher. Vick stirs his coffee with his knife. Claire brings her own food over and sits down with them.

"Look at this, Claire," August says, unfolding the napkin on his lap. "This is great. *The* place to come for a hot meal, obviously."

"You can always come here," Claire says. "You know that."

"So what's new?"

"Nothing—well no, that's not true. Everything's new actually."

Vick nods with her. They obviously talked as he was on his way over.

"I'm trying to make a change," Claire says. "I think it's a change. Maybe it's the same old thing." August knows where this one was going. David, her husband, had been a source of frustration for some time. He is too mousy, she claims, too simpering, and passive and passionless. She wants a man who has some urges, who doesn't always go on what makes logical sense.

"Sure," August says, unsure of what to say. "Um, these

eggs are good." A touch of paprika and cream cheese.

"This guy is pretty clueless," Claire says. "I guess I can still get away with looking younger than I am. I just started going to these socials at the community college."

"Right—"

"And, the third time, the third time was a charm," Claire says. She uses her fingers to flick a nugget of eggs into her mouth. "Met this college guy named Kevin. You know, I'm not even sure what his last name is, and I don't feel guilty."

"That's what she's been saying all morning, August." Vick is already done with his eggs and toast. He smiles at August knowingly.

"Do you actually chew?" August winks. Claire is insistent.

"I'm not, I'm—" Vick runs his fingers through his hair.

"Right, no need to dwell on any—"

"Right, August," Claire says. "That's it."

"That's it?"

"Well, I did tell David. We were sitting there, watching television. I yawned and said that I'm going to bed. As I was walking up the stairs I said 'Oh, and I'm with another man now.' So, goodnight!'"

"What did he say?" August sips his coffee. Manna.

"He shrugged and flipped the channel. Either he doesn't care, or pretended not to. I really am just trying to get a rise out of him. He is the living dead."

"Yeah," August says.

"He's so, there's no *intensity* or anything there. There's very—"

"There's nothing, huh?" August says.

"Not a whole lot. But more than this Kevin kid. It's actually funny. He thinks I'm a college professor—that's what I told him. He couldn't imagine a life outside of his own head. When I take him back here I tell him it's my parents' house, and that if they ever caught me I'd be dead. It's actually pretty hilarious." The three of them smile together and sip their coffee. August feels like a person among people.

They move into the living room and listen to Lester Young blow on the stereo. The living room is furnished in a similar vein. The couches have a dormitory air, big and blocky with tannish weave pillows. The conversation shifts to August, his life, what changes? What news? A light drizzle spatters the windows and roof. The sky is slate gray—the kind only Maryland seems to produce.

"I think my own change came, well you guys know." Vick was supported by his disability check for three years after the warehouse accident. For two of those he literally couldn't work, unless he was home. He was wheelchair bound for six years. Broke both legs. Multiple fractures. "Everything seems fresh, still fresh. I like driving a cab. I actually enjoy it most of the time."

"You seem to," August says.

"I don't know if I was in D.C., but..."

"Yeah, but you've *changed* your life. You have made improvements. You also have a great wife."

"Yeah, I do," he says. "My point is though—"

"Your point is Vick is great," Claire says.

"Yeah—No, my point is why don't you find yourself something you love, August? Something you can't do without."

"My job's okay," August says. "Anyway, too late for that."

"You were Rookie of the Year. I hope you haven't completely blocked that out of your mind. That's *huge.*"

"No, I guess not," August says. "Not completely. I wish I had."

"I mean, you accomplished a lot on a large stage. A whole lot," Vick says.

"Yeah," August agrees. He'd like to shift the conversation away from him again.

"I mean, you have let yourself get completely pinned down. Completely. What the hell are you doing anymore?" Despite the tough love, there is a gentleness in Vick's voice. The rain picks up. The wind flushes against the townhouse, shudders the vinyl siding.

"Hey, you know—"

"No, wait," Vick says. "Why don't you just get a job scouting or something? You're still an ex-athlete. You don't have to be nobody. They could still use your eye. Do something you like to do."

"I don't know, man. I don't know about any of that."

"Don't be so hard on the man, Vick," Claire rubs his arm. "Let him breathe."

"All right, all right. One more thing though, okay?"

"Yeah, what?" August splays his hands on his knees.

"Get a car, would you?"

On the way back August stops at the sight of lichen—the drizzle still speckling his jacket, pinging against his plastic bag. The wind whips through his hair, feels cool against his cheek.

The lichen seems odd to him at this moment, too grayish to be real, some kind of unnatural fuzz—and out of place.

When he went back to Rochester, August grew a beard. He decided on a superstition, like many baseball players. Until he made it back to the majors he wouldn't shave. He wouldn't think about razors even; he would repress some part of himself to achieve a greater good. "I'm coming right back," he said to himself. "I'm coming right back up there. One solid night down here, and I'm back."

His first game for Rochester was no better. When he walked out onto the mound *it* wasn't there—the energy, the desire, the inner burn. He was there because he had no other choice. Thoughts came through him, where he would rather be, what he would rather be doing, anything but pitching a minor league game in front of five thousand. The first inning he walked five, two scored on a single, one scored when he a hit batter in the back, and a double scored two more.

The next inning he gave up a two run homer. He didn't sweat this time; not enough desire for sweat. He wasn't *there*. He thought about snorting coke after the game, but with whom? All the minor leaguers wanted to make it to the bigs; they didn't want to shoot themselves in the foot for something stupid prematurely. The Red Wings players who hadn't been to the majors looked at him with a sense of reverence and awe, and tentative fear—'this is what can happen if you go up and don't get it done.' Right back where you started. The ex-biggies shunned him; he was on the same level as they were. He was dead meat on a downward spiral.

Ultimately August was pulled with two on and one out. So much for a quick comeback. August sat in the locker room, alone, a hot towel over his head—the most desolate man in the world. Nobody patted him on the back, nobody looked at him. He sat there for hours, zoned.

And the rest of his outings were only slightly better, some worse. Seven starts, E.R.A of 6.45, 1-4 record, and it could have been a lot worse. He never made it back up that season. The Red Wings manager wanted him down to double A, thought August wasn't helping his team either. The next year August started in Bluefield, finished up with a 3-11 record, 5.09 E.R.A. As far as the Orioles organization was concerned he was washed up, old history, good as gone. He had trouble even finding coke in the small towns, couldn't afford it anymore. He had to sell his house, live in an apartment alone, in the shabbiest apartment complex there was in town. August began drinking, throwing knives at a dart board, couldn't sleep, no more big buffets at the end of every game. Long bus rides that wore him out. Dingy stadiums, small time. He was small time. The kids were the ones with futures, the kids coming up—the ones that didn't even have to shave. He was dead meat.

And then during the off-season after Bluefield, August shaved. That was the end of it. He dipped his razor into the hot water. He wept, face hot and red. Drunk out of his mind, and flushed. He dipped his razor into the hot water, lathered the shaving cream on his face. Dragged the blade down his face. He could feel the hairs pull. The music blared. Neighbors below and next-door were awake, banging on their ceiling and walls for him to quiet down. The tears dripped into the lather water, and he dragged the razor down his face again. Raw swaths of skin peaked under the flatness of his beard. And he pulled the razor down his face again and again. He would find something new. Life could go a different way; it would have to. He would have to make his own closure, admit successes and failures. There are two kinds of thoughts: the ones that affirm the current structure of your life, and the kinds that change your whole slant. The latter kind were the ones that seemed to dominate August despite himself. And obsess him.

4. Wednesday

In this dream the whole place goes up in flames. It doesn't start in one place; it starts in every place. Spontaneous combustion, and suddenly everything is licking orange, hissing, crackling. That's what he hears first—the *sound* of fire. The crackling sound. No smoke. And where is he? He's trying to discern that. He's not inside, he's floating inside maybe, a ghost, not to be personally harmed, an invisible witness. What's frightening is the abstraction of fire, the consuming nature, humbling—what it can leave behind: everything, everything.

In this dream he does float outside, as his rooms are engulfed. He's watching the apartment complex as if from above. The people inside don't seem to respond or care. They are hypnotized. It's night, and all the cars are in the parking lot, but nobody does anything. And that's when it gets personal. The others, the others. Somebody has to warn them. The dream quickens. He floats up the stairs. He can feel the heat through the stairwell. He knocks on the first door. Nobody answers. Knocks on the second door, and nobody answers. Everyone's asleep. The unknowing and innocent. The bust.

He's up, and in the shower. His shift today is early, eight

to three. He throws his normal lunch in a bag, tightens it, shaves quickly, drinks orange juice, prune juice and scarfs down a banana. He finds Zachary inside room four, talking to a man in a green sweater, polka dotted tie underneath the collar, brown slacks, baby face, cirrus blonde hair, hiking boots the size of pie pans. They both turn to watch him enter and for a moment he knows how Ryan feels.

"Hey there, good morning. Just give me a second will you?"

"Sure thing, sure." The other man smiles politely, and blinks, looks down at his feet. The man's trying to rent a room, for some future arrangement. On his face the uncertain 'Well-this-might-do' quality flashes on and off like a strobe lamp.

"I'll meet you back in the storeroom in five minutes."

As he's making his way down the hall, August knows he will need to buff the floors later. They look flat and lusterless, and he sees dust along the runners. He'll probably have to arrange one room at least, fix the nursery school fence outside, finish the window washing. Those things will fill most of the day. What else is there to life? Filling time until the next thing, then filling that time until the next thing. A never-ending string of filling and emptying.

August places his lunch bag on the shelving, next to the plastic trash bags and cleaners. Ray left everything basically where it should be, although a can of white paint has been opened. August can see that. Ray is in the kitchen touching up the walls, something that's been a secondary part of their list for weeks. Where Ray's style is expansive, and takes all possibilities into account, August chooses one way or another, lives or dies by it. One way or another he'll make his way in life by the intractable insistence of his will. He'll pour the paint into the rolling pan or a small bucket and just bring that. Ray, on the other hand, will surround himself with paint cans.

August thinks about taking one of the chairs from the stack in the storage room, sitting on it, kicking back until Zachary returns to dole out orders. He certainly feels that would be called for. A good power nap. But the shelving needs organizing, the storage room could use a good sweep, some of the paint cans are out of line. August decides to sweep—not enough time to really accomplish the others—and better to achieve one thing than do a sloppy job on something bigger. The dustpan and broom—an instrument that has changed little over the centuries: It's still straw that whisks the majority of the dirt, dead water bugs, crumbs from Ray's dinner, fraying of plastic from the ripped plastic glove from two days ago, residue of dried paint flakes and stray trash escaped through a paper clip hole from the office trash bag.

And as August is putting the broom away, Zachary knocks and enters without pause. His face is more of crescent than his son's, August notices. The chin is more pronounced, lips thinner, teeth glazed yellow—smoker's teeth. When August first came on board he was surprised by how many people of the cloth smoked; he saw some kind of devilish inconsistency there. Zachary has been trying to quit, chews gum, chews coffee stirrers and toothpicks. He lost ten thousand last year on the stock market. It was his decision to layer the building in plants, as if he wanted to cover over his losses with some constrained product of nature.

"I actually wanted to talk to you about my son," he says. Zachary stands a foot too close for comfort, making every conversation feel like a confrontation. August can smell his smoky breath, even through the cinnamon gum aroma.

"Ryan," is all August says.

"What I wanted to say was that I think you did a good job the other night. He's pretty held back, and he's not going to say a lot. And it's not as if I can't tell when something is bothering him. This is something else though."

"Right."

"Right, he seemed happy," Zachary says. "I picked him up and he was saying how you like the Orioles and so on, and so on. He didn't have to sound excited for me to realize what he was talking about."

"What do—"

"Okay, on the phone I actually didn't tell you everything there is to know."

"What's—"

"This is not just a job for him," Zachary says. "You should know that."

"Okay."

"What I mean is he is being *punished* here." August gives no reply to this, not surprised. He has 'reformed' many kids who have come through the door for community service for some infraction or another. August is used to this. The kids in the neighborhood have come to respect him. They clean up the trash around the building because they know if they fail to do it, Mr. August will have to.

"He—well he stole a watch from a store in the mall. The watch was cheap, twenty dollars or something. But he was caught by the video surveillance system. He has to do his time or face a fine, basically. We are all ashamed and he doesn't want to talk about it. So I'm asking for your help."

"So what you're—"

"What I'm saying is I just don't want you to give him any special treatment. Just like the other night. Did it go okay for you?" Maybe he was peeved that they listened to the game together. Maybe he wanted greater constraints.

"Yeah, of course. He's a good kid, a very good kid."

'He wasn't too much of—"

"No, I'll treat him fine," August says. "Don't worry."

"But not *too* good, that's what I'm saying. Tough love."

Once Zachary took August aside and told him earnestly that he considers August part of the ecclesiastical staff here. He's a kind of missionary too, he said. This has something to do with it. Zachary sees him as an appendage.

"One more thing, August...I was hoping you could stay an extra half hour or so to get him started today. He'll be with Ray tonight, but I think you might be better at explaining things initially. Plus you were with him before, so...the transition would be smoother. If you could do that?"

"Sure, no problem at all."

"And of course you'll get the time and a half," Zachary says.

August nods in affirmation.

At exactly three Ryan walks through the front doors. August completes the list, spurred on by some kind of low-grade envy—Ray gets to work with him tonight and not him. At least he gets the half-hour. August dismisses these feelings, but he also can sense them pushing him on towards other tasks. He feels their afterglow.

When Ryan walks in, August is finishing the last panel of the window washing on the far side of the front entrance. Ryan waves across the long corridor and struts back outside and across the courtyard to the exterior door closer to August. He's young, so oblivious and young, August thinks. He's carrying another brown bag dinner, and this time he has a blue thermos as well with a white screw-on cap. They exchange hellos and get onto the business of prepping him for tonight's work. Ray will be in at any minute, and then it will be a battle. He wants to get everything out of the way before that moment. August leads the boy back into the back room. Also a concern: August wants to make sure Ryan acknowledges his errors, and he wants to start that type of training today with an honest exchange.

August tells Ryan that they used to use the old fashioned buffers, but now they have brand new burnishers which run at a higher speed. First you have to replace the drive pad, August says. If you don't do that the floor won't be really clean. Then what you do is spread the detergent solution over the floor—not flooding the floor, not letting the detergent sit too long or the tiles will buckle—and the Interfaith Center will be out thousands. It's important. You spread it thin; a little goes a long way. Then just run the wheels, let it circle, and keep it under wraps so it doesn't whap the walls. That's about it, August says, that's all.

During the whole explanation Ryan seems more accustomed to the idea of being there than he was before. No hat, this time. No scowl. No "Whatever."

"Hey, I'm not going to be working with you tonight," he says. He wrinkles the upper cuff of the bag in and out.

"Huh?"

"Not tonight, Ryan."

"Hey, can we use your radio when you leave?"

"Sure you can, Ryan."

When Ray gets there, August helps them start the vacuuming. When they're in the back room he turns to Ray and says, "He's all yours, man," but Ray doesn't seem to hear. The vacuum's too loud. All the better.

Even though it's a cool evening and he's tired, August decides to go fishing after work. His favorite spot is Wilde Lake, on the pier. He sits on the edge of the pier as before, this time with his mini-rod and box of worms. Of course it's not about catching anything. It's about losing yourself in an activity that people see as relaxing (and maybe it is). Usually August believes it is.

He sits for hours, dangling the line in the water, not knowing what will happen next, if anything at all. He doesn't just mean fishing. The twists of life sometimes seem slight, until he looks at the larger picture. When he was a professional athlete who would have thought he'd be tutoring the boss's son to the ways of janitorial skills? Who would have thought the same man who had a different woman every night would be so alone now? Who could have predicted that he'd be living down the street from his brother and sister who he disregarded during his moment in the limelight? The twists that have occurred in his life are twists upon themselves.

As he's sitting around listening to the game on the radio, August receives a phone call.

"Hey, man, it's your brother," probably calling to take the bite off the earlier statements he made. "Just taking a break to call you, really."

"Hey, man."

"Yes. Listen, you probably know why I'm calling."

"I have a guess."

"I bet. Just wanted to make sure you didn't think I was out to tell you how to live, that's all. I don't have the map to God."

"Yeah, I know," August says. "No, it's—you're kicking my ass. What I need. It's a good thing really. I'm in some kind of sleep these days."

"Something like that," Vick says. "Doesn't matter. You're living. Hey, listen. There was something I did want to tell you though. I just heard this today."

"What's that?"

"This couple jumped in my cab this afternoon," Vick says.

"Right."

"And they were just nice. Just a nice couple. They mentioned they said they were renting out a room in their house. Just thought you might want to know about it. You don't have to do anything about it though. Just thought you might want to know, in case you want to make a change."

August tells his brother he appreciates it and that maybe a change *is* in order.

"Just, you know. I care… Don't feel like anybody's ashamed of anything, or anything like that."

"I don't think that," August says. "I don't think that at all. If anything you're looking out for me. Who else is doing that?"

"That's, that's what I'm saying. You have to—"

"I know do it for—"

"Do it for yourself, that's what I'm saying." August knows when intentions are good you can't stray too-too far from the real path.

"You're trying hard, man. I appreciate that," August says.

At 8:30 August decides to walk back up to the Interfaith Center. The Orioles are actually winning two to nothing, so he feels he can justify his trip by sharing the good news with Ryan, who may or may not know. But he should know.

The courtyard is a circle of yellow. The air is actually warmer than it was during the day. In the strange flux of spring these things can happen. The building looks smaller than he remembers in the shadows and light. The construction of the building was early seventies minimalism, anti-establishment. August thinks it looks squashed, like somebody sat on a hat. Governor Warfield Parkway is quiet. Two people stand in the shadows by the willow tree box, talking in whispers. August wears his slacks and a brown jacket over his button-down country-style shirt. And he walks towards the building, sucking on his inner cheek.

He can't see Ray or Ryan anywhere. They must be in the office, doing the rounds. August walks straight in the main entrance; doesn't want to seem like he's sneaking around, watching. But the office is locked and dark. The building is quiet, no distant vacuum or sounds of cleaning, or even a baseball game. August circles around the corridor, past rooms three and four—both black—to the kitchen. No signs there either. He loops back to the storeroom, expects to find them there organizing or sitting around shooting the shit, but they're not there either. Then it hits him where they are: outside, in back, working on that fence that he didn't finish. It's warm enough and light enough to do it. As he passes by the plants, he runs his fingers through their tendrils and he walks towards the nursery room. And he sees them outside the door. He speeds up, opens the door. And they are both—Ryan and Ray—smoking cigarettes.

"Hey, what are you two doing?"

"Hey, Duke," Ray says, exhaling in a burst of smoke and breath. Why is it that smokers have such a sense of casual camaraderie? August used to understand. Ryan takes a draw, offers one to August. Shit, August thinks.

"First of all..." August says. In his mind, he's trying to decide how hard he should come down; he feels responsible for Ryan; his father came to him personally. "Ryan, you shouldn't be doing that here, at work. You shouldn't be smoking. Under age and all. I can't be held responsible."

"Duke, it's okay, it's okay. *I'm* right here," Ray says.

"Yeah I can see that pretty clear," August says. "What are you, the smoking supervisor?"

"Don't worry about it," Ray says. "What are you doing here anyway, man?" Ryan looks away and August watches him. It's as if he thinks he shouldn't be there, as if it was his parents in front of him arguing about sex or money, or his college fund. Or as if he can't deal with both men at the same time, too much overload—people who shouldn't be in the same place at the same time.

"I was bored, wanted to take a walk that's all. Plus, I don't need to explain. I *work* here, don't I?"

"That was very nice of you to stop by, August. But we've got everything under control, it seems." He never calls August 'August.'

"What did you call me?"

"'August,' Duke."

He tells Ray *he's* ultimately responsible. The boss put *him* in charge, specifically. "So it's my problem."

Ray shrugs. So put them out, August says and Ryan lets his cigarette drop to the pad of concrete. Clears his throat.

"And Ryan."

"Yeah?"

"The Orioles are winning. Thought you might be listening."

"Are they?"

"Yeah, three to one." August lets the door swing closed, filled with ambivalence. He swooshes past Ray and Ryan, through the picket gate and around right through the wet grass and moonlight.

5. Thursday

Fifteen years later the Interfaith Center would throw a retirement service for Ray and August, together. They would sit next to each other and elbow each other when the pastors and rabbis reminisced about the time the speaker system in room two broadcasted the Baptist choir into the Unitarian service, or when they had to store that huge x-ray machine for the Maryland chemists conference, or how Ray and August both rushed out to shovel the snow any time it fell, as it fell, no matter what.

Zachary would stand up and give a long laudatory speech about how "solid" both janitors were, how they serviced the community in so many ways, how they also spread the word of God in whatever form it needed to be spread, in their own way, how they were honest, and good, and hardworking, and how these are the kinds of traits they passed on to the young people who were sometimes in their care. Ryan would drive five hours to proclaim how much he learned from those two, the difference it made to his life. August would notice that Ryan had his father's tendencies for melodrama and sentimentality and borderline histrionics, that Ryan seemed rickety up there, pieced together by a thread. Ryan would say he *grew.* He really grew. August would think, but did he really? And what percentage of his pie graph would be filled with disillusionment?

The wife of Bradley York, the current manager, would give a history of the time the two men spent at the Interfaith Center. The hundred people in the service would sing along to "What a Friend We Have in Jesus," and slow the final line down to a rollicking praise: "*Thou wilt find a sol-ace there.*" They would listen to prayers and scripture from a priest and a reverend. They would receive gifts including designer hats and sweaters, plane tickets to Europe, food, and more food, music, plaques, medals, honors. Above and beyond the Rookie of the Year award, it would be August's proudest moment. He would look back and think I'm glad I refrained from listening to my brother about changing jobs. No way. No way.

All morning August couldn't get Kelly Frank out of his head—

the little girl he hit when he was drunk. Before he left his car on the side of the road, the keys in the ignition, doors unlocked, for anybody to take. It was two weeks before it was gone, and it could have been the police who eventually took it. August didn't care. As long as he got rid of the machine. It was the car that did it. It was out of his control.

It had only been two months since he moved back to Columbia, from the road, his baseball career over. He didn't work at all, lived off the money he made as a player, until it ran dry. August blew his time drinking and playing cards with Byron, Mikie, and Will, people he met at the pub. And that night they had been up watching porn flicks in Baltimore, going to strip clubs, coming back and drinking more with the hooker in Will's basement bedroom.

At seven thirty in the morning August decided he'd better return home, drunk, smelling of cigarettes, sweat, sex. When he saw the school bus stopped in front of him on Governor Warfield, he didn't care what he had to do to get by it, and he turned his radio up. The line of children started towards the bus, and Kelly was the first in line. August didn't see them; he was already home in his own mind. He blew past the blinking red lights, and as he passed the plane of the bumper, he saw the little girl look right at him, her brown eyes, her dark brown hair, skin the color of a walnut, heard her little body hit the bumper, saw her flip up into the early morning air in an arc above him, in front of him—thirty feet up into the air the newspaper said, one hundred feet out. He slammed on his brakes right before he reached her body on the asphalt. There was no blood anywhere, but he turned his head back towards the bus.

And the parents and children ran. The bus driver clambered out of his seat. They were running towards him, over the one hundred feet, yelling, screaming, hair whipping in the breeze, and it was as if he was back at Memorial Stadium, the crowd on its feet, watching his every move, watching him, hollering. He has watched those children and adults in slow motion, every step they made, the contortions developing on their faces, the colors vivid, the smell of rain in the air, the clouds gray and heavy above him, the slightest breeze through the trees, the smell of burnt rubber, the radio playing "I Can't Get No...I Can't Get No," the smells on him, sex, sweat, booze. Still drunk.

He sniffled. He didn't know if it was the coke, but his nose itched. He wiped it with the back of his hand, and then the people were all around. Someone pushed him out of the way. The others didn't stop at him; they rushed to the girl, surrounded her. Someone yelled for an ambulance. Someone started CPR on the body. One of the mothers ran back past him, down the sidewalk. One of her shoes fell off, and she kept running, the shoe falling into the road in front of the bus. Nobody said a word to him, but they all looked at him, as they held the girl on the ground. He couldn't leave and didn't. Someone held his arm. The sirens came, including two police cruisers, and that was when his life changed. That was when he called Vick, asked him to bail him out, when he dumped his car on the side of the road, and went to jail for ten years (reduced to five ultimately) — manslaughter, among other charges. And he hasn't driven a car since, and vows not to. Never, never.

"Hey, Ryan," August says. It's three o'clock. He's pushing a broom, which he tries to do twice a day, just to keep everything looking neat. It only takes fifteen minutes.

"How's everything going?"

"Pretty good, I guess."

"What are you up to?"

"Besides smoking, not enough probably. My Dad grounded me again last night, and said I have to work here longer since I smoked. I guess he smelled it on me. I didn't tell him Ray was there."

"Oh." August props himself against the broom. He's not going to play the wise man. "Hey, I have something for you, back in the storage room."

"Okay," the kid says.

"Okay? Let's go." August props the broom against the corridor wall, walks with Ryan back to the room. Inside it's darker. He hands the boy a shoebox.

"What's this?" Ryan puts his dinner into the space previously occupied by the box.

"Open it." He does, ripping the tape off the sides with his teeth, pulling the lid right off. The smell comes out first, summery, verdant—strawberries. And then Ryan sees them, and a can of Pepsi.

"They're good berries too because I went to the health food store for them. And I knew you liked that soda, right?"

"Right." Ryan sits down on one of the excess chairs, as if he has to weigh the significance. He picks a strawberry from the box, asks August if he wants one.

"No, they're yours. Wash them first though."

"You're here tonight, right?"

"Right," August says. "Is that okay with you?"

"I think so," he says, and pops up with the box of strawberries to wash them off. The way his ears flare back, August knows the kid is smiling.

For dinner Ryan has leftover macaroni and cheese, with carrot sticks, and a bag of potato chips. His can of Pepsi is tepid. August has beans and rice, and potato bread, and an orange, with orange juice. They are back in the kitchen together, with only the oven light on so they can see if the roach motels worked.

"This is a pretty orange dinner," Ryan says. "You have an orange and orange juice. I have carrots and macaroni. We didn't spread our colors around very good."

"You're right," August says, watching the floor. Nothing.

"Why are you, uh, I mean, *nice* to me?"

"I don't really feel like I am, but I guess I'm trying to be," August says. "This is just normal."

The boy says that's what he doesn't get at all, and he'd like August to try to explain these things to him: why people do the things they do.

"That's a hard thing to know isn't it? There really is no way of knowing for sure, one way or another."

"I guess not. Don't know."

"Son, there are, things. I have things that—we all have these things—that I haven't told you, that lots of people don't know. For me, that has a lot, a lot to do with it."

"Like what?"

"Well for one I have been in prison. Did you know that? Your father may have told you."

"Really?"

"I hurt somebody badly and I had to be punished for it. It did help get me together, closer to where I am now than I was, that's for sure."

He tells the kid about life in prison, which he shapes as much to scare the kid, as to inform him. August answers his questions—how long, when, where. He avoids the worst of the worst though.

"And what I wanted to tell you really was I also was a professional baseball player. In case that is of interest to you."

"You were?"

"1963-1966. You have a baseball history book?"

"No," Ryan said, riveted.

"I won Rookie of the Year in 1963. Look it up."

"What's your last name?"

"Griffin."

Then he relays stories about those days, how his career took off, and ended. August again tried to provide some kind of moral—that he squandered his life.

"Yeah, but wait, you won Rookie of the Year! That's big."

"Who cares? Long time ago. Look, son. I just want to explain to you—I don't want to see you anywhere near some of the places I used to hang out."

"Where were those places?"

"I'm not telling you. That's the point." August peals his orange, fills the whole room with citrus scent. Ryan says he's trying to be good, and that it's partly that his Dad and Mom aren't getting along. He says he needs an outlet sometimes.

"Is that what was with the smoking then?"

"I don't know. Like you said, it's hard to explain why people do the things they do."

"You're right," August says. "I just don't want to ever see you do that again around me."

"Deal," Ryan says.

"Deal."

August says he has an extra copy somewhere on this damn key chain. He's got about a hundred on there, each one practically identical. Most of them are labeled. He inherited these keys from the janitor before him, Earl Hanes, who retired. August did have to replace the labels as they peeled off, as they became unreadable. And what Earl Hanes told him before he left for good was make it fun, make the work fun somehow and you can get by. If you start thinking about it, he said, then you'll start thinking about how *little* it means. That's true of everything, he said, not just janitorial things. Good advice.

On the way back from eating, the kid says locking up must be the easy part about the job. No way, August says. It's one of the most difficult parts of the job. You gotta get used to those locks. A lock is a lock, the kid says. Not these locks, August says. These locks are different. So he stops at the closest door and demonstrates from the inside, a turn to the left to clear the bolt, a turn to the right, and a turn all the way back to the left, hard, and clicking it. There's gotta be a better way, Ryan says. Well, what's the better way then? August shakes his head. I don't know. Ryan says he'd try it from the outside. He takes the key, and with one swift turn, the door is locked and he can't get back in through the door. Ha! He walks back around through the next one, smiling in challenge.

"So here it is," August says. "Here's the key." He hands

the piece of metal to Ryan in the storeroom. Ryan takes it between his thumb and forefinger, and holds it by his fingertips. Ryan asks why he's giving it to him. Is he supposed to open something for him?

"No, we're locking up now. And I have an idea."

"What's that?"

"Follow me." They burst out of the room at a quick pace, walk down the hall alone. "We'll leave the front door open, but we do have to lock up, and I'm going to show you how it's done."

"Okay." August stops them in front of one of the doors. He takes out the key and holds it in front of Ryan.

"This is the master key. It opens all the doors to the building."

"Okay."

"You can go on the outside. I'll stay inside, and we'll see who can finish first."

"I don't understand."

"You go first, and I'll time you, and then I'll go, and uh, you can time me. We'll see who can finish first."

"Okay."

"Okay, okay." So Ryan goes outside, walks to the far end of the outside glass, stands at attention. He waves. August waves back, smiling, points to his watch, waits until it circles around to the twelve. To himself: on your mark, get set, go! And he drops his hand, points to Ryan. And Ryan rushes down the line, locking, locking, locking, locking, locking. No check, no stop and make sure everything's clear. The kid makes it all the way down the line in two minutes, and back inside, asking how much time. August shakes his head in mock dismay, saying

"Over half an hour at least. No way I can beat that." And he knows the second part of that is true.

That night August saw a part of his dream he never saw before. It was after all the flames burnt out. He was in a field somewhere, surrounded by trees on all sides, somewhere he's never been before. The air was still, and the moonlight was so bright he woke up. He was in a tent, and could smell the polysynthetic fibers, the plastic. He unzipped the tent, and crawled out into the night. It was warm; he could feel that. He started walking towards the woods. In this dream he was not afraid. The woods held no sense of foreboding, and he walked right into them. August could smell the pine, and oak, and poplar. It seemed like any patch of woods. And he kept walking into the woods. He felt he had to. No choice in the matter at all. Inside the woods he came to a clearing, and he looked around the clearing and there it was in the middle of the clearing—a tent, just like the tent he left, and he walked up to it. And inside the tent, there he was asleep with the moonlight dousing him.

6. Friday

And what exactly is it about this kid that makes August contemplate and consider? He's not sure. The shower feels right, the way the water smells, the hardness of the water—if that's it? The shampoo he uses is the same shampoo he has always used, a generic honey blend from the grocery store. Everyone has their habits, and he has his. What else is there to keep us together, and apart? August blinks his eyes closed in the shower, smelling the soapy, sweet smell. He's done with washing. He's allowing himself to relax and be apart from things. This is what the team psychologist used to talk about when he was a player. It's okay to let your guard down sometimes. Just subsist.

August doesn't look at the bust this morning; he feels the contours of the face this time. The hollowed holes of the eyes, the lips that remind him of cucumber skin, and the smooth polish of the cheeks, the cheek bones, the chin. Maybe what the bust has given him is distraction. Is this the time when he actually addresses the basic elements of his life? And what would that really mean anyway? Is that what Ryan is for? Is he toiling to earn himself a reprieve? August doesn't have the answers, although he feels different somehow, and that in itself is something.

Breakfast is the usual: he shaves; he makes a lunch for himself. At 7:30 in the morning August can hear others outside, starting their cars, walking down the corridor, ready to join the work force, their own part of it. August likes feeling this kind of routine camaraderie, as if he actually is part of a larger society. Before it was not this way. Before, he thought he could do it all, and the lives that other people lead were too abstract—and maybe *better*, maybe that was it—for him to really relate or care at all. Maybe he has spent all these years wallowing in himself too long, maybe Ryan is here to make him realize that fact. Even if it's not *entirely* true, he thinks, there is some truth to it.

So much is under the surface, and what you see is just part of what, in the long run, is important. The iceberg floats along, August knows. But then, part of this camaraderie is realizing that everyone is like this. Everyone has regrets, and disappointments and has failed miserably at something. He is no different. His life has just been played-out more directly, more vividly. His mistakes arrived early.

August is out the door, and walking to work, the early shift after the late shift last night—too much, too much. And what he considers this morning is unexpected, but perhaps it shouldn't be surprising considering recent patterns. His father bubbles into his brain. August walks.

Before the trip the last time August saw his father was in 1979. August was in Columbia by then, working exactly where he is working still, but his father was in Florida, living in the Keys by himself as he had since August's mother died of ovarian cancer. Too early, too young. August was twelve. He hated his father for that, hated anyone who would drop out of society. A ghost.

But last year his father told him on the phone he had arrhythmia and had been taking medication for years. He said that it was bad enough that the doctors believed he could have a life-ending heart attack within the next six months. High blood pressure. His father started drinking to *slow* himself, but that made it worse. His father wanted to make sure he saw his son before that happened, if that happened. He said he had some money he wanted to spend on August, and he just wanted August to fly down to Miami and then they'd figure it out. He'd pay for the ticket.

When August arrived at the airport his father was drunk, playing gin rummy on the airport floor with a teenager. His father was wearing a trench coat, and purple shorts underneath. He had his back turned to the terminal, and was almost in the middle of the corridor looking foolish. His neck was half-shaved, and he wore a white tank top with flip flops, drinking out of a thermos to cloak the booze. He probably peppered the rum with eggnog. His father was a successful bank executive for years, retired at the age of fifty. If he wanted to live a sordid life, that was his own affair. The man has been through a lot; give it to him. But to make his problems so glaringly public?

August sat on one of the nearby airport seats, bag in hand. He watched his father and this boy play cards.

"I'll tell you, the most important part of life is *family*. What else is there really?"

"Fun man, fun goes a damn long way," the boy said. "Fucking get drunk, get high, get laid. Live life."

"No, no, no. I'm telling you. It does go a long way, but family goes longer."

"You have a—"

"Oh yeah, oh yeah. Come on." The boy tilted his head askew, trying to sneak a look at his father's cards. The plane heading for Dallas was loading. She had a nasally voice, and the system cracked a little, it seemed, under the weight of her voice. August could smell pretzels and popcorn from the nearby stand. His father did a good job of masking the smell on his breath. Not a trace. "What do you think I'm here for? My health?"

"Obviously not, since you're spinning out of your mind."

"I'm not? How old are you anyway?"

"Me, I'm eighteen. I'm not stupid, man."

"Okay, that's—give me my cards back. You're trying to get a look anyway."

He snapped back.

"No, no. I'm not giving you shit, man."

"You'll give me the damn—"

And that's when August jumped in, with his drunk father chasing after some punk kid for a few squares of laminated paper.

"Oh good," his father said. Then he turned back to the kid with the ridiculous flasher trench coat, and mussed hair. "See, this is the reason I'm here. *Family.*"

"I'm keeping these cards."

"Why don't you shove them up your mother's ass?"

"What did you say? You said—"

"Stupid punk." August had to physically stand between the two of them, tell the kid he could have the cards, take the cards, and practically carry his father to the car— when they finally found it. In his state his father couldn't remember where he parked for the life of him. They walked through nearly every airport parking lot trying to find his black Caddy. Then in Lot FF, his father remembered he *sold* the Cadillac.

"That's right," he said. "I took the bus," which August took to mean, he rode the bus. But his father meant he *bought* a bus, a big purple bus. He had to stop and sit on the rear bumper of somebody's Fairlane. He pulled out his keys.

"It used to be a prison bus, until I bought it. That's right." He drooled. When they finally got to lot Y, the bus was parked across five parking spots, and his father sat down, then laid down, and fell asleep on the first bench seat in. And August waited until he woke up, and then drove both of them back to his father's house on the island, surrounded by the Caribbean, like a sky of water.

"I was going to take you to Mexico," his father said the

next night. His skin looked tired, and he seemed to be losing hair—August found clumps of it here and there, on the sofa, on the rug, on the kitchen counter. "But we can just stay here if you want."

They were in a sports bar with framed baseball photographs surrounding them, some autographed, some not, baseball bats, jerseys, plaques inset with baseball cards, some autographed, some not, covers of magazines and posters, some autographed, some not. Roger Clemens. Sandy Koufax. Bob Gibson. Steve Carlton. Ron Guidry. Greg Maddux. Nolan Ryan.

"We're in a sports bar, Dad? I don't know how happy I am about this, at all."

"Oh, laugh it up. It's just people. We're all people."

"Some are more people than others."

"Hey, I'll buy you another margarita." And he did. The waitress came by, the one who said she'll go by Binky. When she pointed to her button August said, "You've got to be kidding." Even in his most ludicrous days, things were never that ludicrous, he thought. Or if they were, he didn't realize it.

"How are you tots doing?"

"Fine, sugar pie," his father said. "What kind of margaritas you guys have now?"

She rattled off a selection of fifteen choices.

"We'll take two lemon-limes," he said, ordering for his son.

"Great, greatty-great."

"I even have the tickets," he said after their waitress left. "But I don't know how much you'd want to go to Cancun."

"I'd be fine with that, Dad."

"No, you'd have too much fun making me feel guilty for spending too much money." They didn't say a word to each other until the margaritas came, and even then the only thing they asked each other was "is it okay?" and "yes." When they were done he ordered two more of the same, only cherry this time. August said he didn't want another sip.

"Why go to Mexico, when we can just stay here and get tanked?"

"Dad, that's not really what I had in mind."

"Who cares what *you* had in mind. You're visiting me on my request. And you're my son. Do what you're told and drink up and have some damn fun. Loosen up." But by one thirty in the morning August was still sitting there, listening to his father's stories, which he had heard before, all of them. Ella dropped by the table then, wearing shorts that barely covered her tush and a lacy-white blouse sans bra, and a big black belt cinching the whole package. August's father kissed her hand, and she sat down next to him.

"Mella Ella!"

"Franky!"

"This, this man sitting across from us was once the Rookie of the Year in the major leagues. Get that?"

"Wow, big boy. You must be proud," she said.

"No, not at all." She giggled, as if she thought he was being modest. His father laughed. Her teeth looked flat, as if they were ground by a millstone.

"Would you like to join us for some other rounds of drinks, back at the castle?" His father could barely keep his eyes open, but he had another drink on the way.

"Sure, big boy."

"Sure, big boy," August said. He asked her how much? She put her finger to her lips and whispered that his father was a steady. Discount.

And when they got back to his mansion on the island, August told him to sit at the breakfast bar in the kitchen, and not to move.

"We need to thank this lovely lady for driving us both home," he said.

"Thank you," August said. He slouched on the chair and tucked his head into his shoulder. The aura of bad-tidings was building. Ella licked her lips and snapped open his father's belt. August was too drunk himself to react, or think about what was happening. And then his father undressed himself, and Ella. August half-watching, half-asleep, glassy eyed. His father's hands were splayed across her bare back, as he leaned her down onto the table. He had crud underneath his fingernails. She had crumbs in her hair. They swiveled back and forth in the shadows.

Stain removals are on the list today. Zachary organizes jobs by theme: painting days (or weeks), floor cleaning, dusting (the whole building), exterior maintenance—mowing the grass, raking leaves, weeding the garden—fixing electronic equipment, kitchen detail. Fridays are usually for plants, and dusting. August walks around the building with a large jug, and a sprayer, pours water into each potted plant. This is one of his favorite duties, and he is tempted to do it more than once a week. Maybe he'll ask about that. If he's in a hurry, he'll carry the plants to the baptismal, and then splash water from there into the plants, but then he knows the drain clogs with leaves, and in the end it's more work.

In Rabbi Segal's office there is a coffee stain on the white sofa cushion. For this, August knows, you use a cleaning solvent—a solution of one half teaspoon liquid detergent, one tablespoon vinegar, one quart water, and then if that doesn't work the enzyme prewash, or alcohol. He prepares the solvent in a bucket and walks though the office to the Rabbi's room— which is locked and empty. In front of the sofa, he bends, kneels, and dabs the fabric with his sponge. He wets his sponge again, watching the fizzle on the sponge; he squeezes the sponge. He will soak the stain for as long as it takes and after an hour the stain has retreated to a distant memory.

In the nursery there are fruit juice stains of the highest order: fruit punch, grape juice, cranberry juice. August uses the same solution for these juice stains, but maybe Zachary didn't see the grass stains by the exterior door. For this the process is more complex: sponge with the solvent and let it dry, sponge with nail polish remover and flush with cleaning solvent, sponge with water and vinegar, sponge with wet spotter and flush with water. This takes time, especially on a light gray rug. He has to ask Zachary if that's what he wants to be done. August leaves the solvent and sponges, walks back into the office, and knocks on Zachary's door.

"Come in."

"Hi, I—"

"Yes, August."

"I was wondering—"

"Yes," Zachary's head is buried in some papers. His desk is covered with a stapler, folders, envelopes, ledger book, staples and paper clips.

"I was wondering. You know those stains in the nursery. They have grass stains back there too."

"Oh, okay."

"You can go ahead and take care of them too, right?"

"Yes sir, no problem at all." Zachary blinks. Outside his window a woman walks her dog along the sidewalk, towards the street. Cars pass by, and the windshields catch the sun. Birds twitter in the trees, out of sight.

"Hey, August?"

"Yes."

"You still don't drive?"

"No sir, I don't drive at all," August says.

"Would you consider driving though, if you, if somebody did a favor for you?"

"I don't think that's possible." August slips his hand in his pocket. He can feel the lump of keys in them. He can feel the cool metal through the fabric.

"Because—well I told you Ryan likes you. I bought two tickets to tomorrow's Orioles game. I wasn't going to mention it until Ryan said something, but that's what I did." August doesn't know what to make of this at all. It suddenly feels like what he should do, but in no way is he ready to do it. This is a crossing. He needs to evaluate, and consider where he's going. Does he want to alter everything he's done before? His face feels heavy, and the sounds outside seem louder. He can hear the dog bark at the birds, at the cars, at the rays of sunlight streaming down through the trees and behind the walls.

"I don't think so," August says. And it feels instinctual, worn into the way he is. The measure of instinct is greater than intuition, and that's a fine line.

"Are you sure? Have you been to the new stadium?"

"No." The team has offered him free seating, invitations to old-timer games.

"Well, you should go. You know about the new stadium. It's nice. It's not the same one anymore, you know." Now Zachary seems to be pointing him in the right direction, addressing the real concerns that August has. He won't have to go back to the haunt, Zachary means.

"I don't think I can." He decides he'll wait to take care of the grass stains until Ryan arrives.

"Oh."

"I'll need to get some nail polish remover and vinegar from the store."

"Sure. Five bucks should cover that, don't you think?"

"That seems about right." Zachary goes to the moneybox. He hands August the money and August nods.

When he walks up through the Village Center to the store, August passes the café where he sat and ate a few days ago. How much has changed since then? It seems like a lot, but maybe it isn't. Maybe he should go to the game, but drive too? It seems like overload. He doesn't even have a valid license anymore. He didn't mention that to Zachary, although Zachary must know, or not care at all. What would be so bad about going? It would probably be fine. He would enjoy himself. He listens to the games. What is one more step?

August enters the grocery store. This isn't a fear, he thinks. I walk into grocery stores every day. Why do I have to be hung up on some place? It's just a place. We're all *people*. I don't have to have any kind of attachments to the place, to anything. I'm just a person going to see a game, and maybe I'd enjoy it, too. Nobody would know who I am, or was. Maybe it would be okay after all.

When Zachary pulls in with Ryan they're both grinning. They don't say anything. August is scrubbing an oil stain from the parking lot with a wire brush. The air is clear and warm, and it feels like spring. Ryan sits down on the curb next to him. Zachary tells them he'll be back in his office if they have any questions about anything.

"It's stain day today," August says.

"Miserable?"

"No, it's a challenging part of the job, actually. I like it." Ryan smiles as if he knows something hidden and elusive. August ignores this, scrapes the asphalt. He's using the heavy work gloves for this job. He had to trudge up to the hardware store and buy the gloves when he needed to hack the bushes and thickets in back. He remembers these sorts of details.

"Do you like your job?"

"I think so," August says. "Why? What do you think?"

"I don't think you do, totally," Ryan says. His voice is straight on, exposed. August scrapes faster.

"No, no. That's not what I meant. I meant, what do *you* think of the job?"

"Oh, it's okay. But you know why I'm here. It's better than I thought."

"Well that's good, right?"

"It's good," Ryan says. "It's good. Hey, so you heard the Orioles won last night?"

"Yeah, I heard something like that," August says. He says he's going to take a break. He never takes breaks, but he needs to now he says. Something doesn't feel exactly right. He sits next to the boy. The curb is cooler than he expects.

"I really want to be like you were," Ryan says. He's looking at his feet. "I think that sometimes." The toes of his work boots are touching. He bites his fingernail off, and spits it onto the asphalt.

"I didn't do anything."

"You won Rookie of the Year. I looked it up. It's true. The book even had your picture in it. You looked like my age or even younger."

"I was young. I was very young."

"I'm young. I just think it's okay to shoot for something. And if you don't get there then at least you tried." August puts his hands on his knees, and thinks about that. That's the best thing anybody's said to him recently. That's exactly what he should be thinking.

"That's a good thing to say," August admits.

"So how about this Orioles game? Will you go with me to this game? My dad already said he told you. Just come with me, okay."

"I don't know," August says.

"I want you to come. It will be fun."

"Fun?"

"Yeah, it'll be fun."

"How will we get there?"

"You can drive, can't you?"

August examines the concrete. "I'll think about it," he says.

7. Saturday

August parks a mile away, under the ramp that leads up to 395. The car is Zachary's. Zachary trusts him this much. August drove for this. Ryan doesn't know the significance. No license, decades of rust. August *drove*. For this kid, for this game.

Ryan pops his seat belt off and practically leaps out of the car. "It's my second car anyway," Zachary said. "Clara's car." August didn't realize they were that much on the outs, but Zachary confessed she's with her sister in Richmond, and he doesn't know when she's returning. When he said this August knew he *had* to go to the game. He, for once, had nothing to lose. The car's a black sports car, and the interior is spotless, and the bumper sticker on the back reads "Life Is A Beach." Sun-faded. August never met this woman. He would have remembered her, for sure.

As they walk up the stairs and walkway leading by the endless parking lot to the distant stadium, Ryan tells August about the other times he's been to games. "This one is the first day game though," he says. "There aren't many day games left." It's 3:35 and the game starts at 3:55, the twilight game. It's only seventy degrees. August wears a pullover hat and his pea coat in case the temperature really drops. Ryan wears an Orioles cap, an Orioles jacket, and has leather gloves with "Orioles," written up the palm. This must affect the grip, August thinks. As they approach the stadium others join in the filing and Ryan seems even more excited. There are so many things August could tell him.

"I brought my baseball cards. Do you mind if we stay afterwards and try to get autographs?" August already knew about this possibility. Zachary was very thorough. August feels like he's doing the right thing suddenly. The light is still clean and wintry, and August knows the shadows will be torture on the batters today.

"Sure, Ryan. No problem."

The seats they have are right under the brim of the overhang in the shade, in the mezzanine.

"If it rains we'll be okay," Ryan says.

August feels uneasy at first. He's on the wrong side of the fence, but it can't be any other way. So much time has passed, and what has he done with himself? The air feels right though—that certain electricity runs through the crowd; something is about to *happen*. The vendors yell out for popcorn, Coke, beer; the scoreboard shows highlights from yesterday; a flock of birds flies silently above them all, and the sun sinks behind a cloud. The P.A. announcer starts into the lineups. The fans boo the Tigers half-heartedly. They cheer for their favorite players, and stand for the national anthem, and take off their hats and place their hats in the middle of their chests—they can't remember if it should be right or left. The Orioles run out to take their positions and the fans clap. The game starts. August buys popcorn for both of them and they scoop handfuls into the hollows of their coats.

August has decided he wants the Orioles to lose, although on television he always roots for them quietly. He would rather have the kid suffer a disappointment. This isn't television. Television is a sliver of the game, August knows, but sometimes a sliver is enough. August doesn't tell the kid he's rooting against the Orioles; he'll keep it to himself and try to have fun, as the kid said. As the Orioles and Tigers exchange one-two-three innings, August and Ryan listen to a father and son argue about what the boy should or shouldn't want from the vendors and concession stands. The boy points to the peanut man and asks if he can have some, whines about the cotton candy, and soda man. The father finally buys a Coke, and says he'll split it with the boy. The boy says he wants his own, but the father says he's not getting that.

"What a brat," Ryan whispers.

As the soda vendor is turning away to make another sale, the father shouts out: "Tell the other guys not to come to this section anymore. We've had enough."

"Sometimes I am glad I never had kids," he says. An inning later the kid drops the soda and it splatters all over Ryan's jeans. The father apologizes, tells his son to apologize— and he does—and gets napkins from one of the hot dog vendors, who he thanks. He gives the napkins to Ryan, and apologizes again. Ryan says it's no big deal, but the father offers to buy him a pretzel. Ryan says no. For a moment August thinks Ryan will agree. By the third inning the score is still zero-zero, and fans are still filing in with rested weekendy faces, sexed, and overfed from the suburbs. August has to duck around and peer through the constant flow of traffic to see anything at all.

In the bottom of the fourth the Tiger pitcher walks two and the Orioles' shortstop hits a three run homer. The fans explode, stopping whatever else they were doing to dance along to the thumping music. The scoreboard flickers. This is so much different from the way things used to be. But that's what they are like. You can't do anything about what you can't do anything about. A group of college kids sits behind August and Ryan, each one carrying a plastic cup of beer. One of the group catches August's eye and says, "Hey, man." August tries to figure out how he should respond to that, and he decides to tip his cap, and he does. They burst out laughing, but maybe they'd be more polite with a touch of humor. They order three rounds of beer, and they are loud enough that one woman blurts out: "Shhhh, we're watching a game."

"What is this, a library?" The woman doesn't say anything.

In the top of the fourth Detroit scores three on a bases loaded single, and a balk. The next inning the Orioles score one on an error by the second baseman. A man was on third. The Orioles are up one by the seventh inning stretch.

"How are you doing?" Ryan asks him. August isn't sure. The crowd is pampered, annoying and distracting. But August has to admit, he feels like a part of society again, where drinks are spilled, where people complain and don't always get along. He just needed out of stuffy, Utopian Columbia—that's probably it. The public life.

"I'm good, I think."

"What do you think of this stadium?"

"It's...different," he says. "It's nice. It's smaller than it looks on television."

"Uh-huh." Ryan asks him if he's still going to drop off a note in the front office. August had actually forgotten. He says he might. They both stand as the John Denver song plays, and people clap and stomp and watch themselves on the video screen. "Thank God I'm a Country Boy!" The façade shadows across the field, cutting across the infield from third to second, now. On the video screen people duck from the camera, or dance like lunatics, and wave signs. August can see his own breath.

"What was the best game you ever pitched?" Ryan asks. "Do you remember?" August has to think about that one. In his mind, his first game will always be the best, the most memorable. Even though he lost the game three to two. He did pitch a two hit shutout his rookie year, against Cleveland. But August tells him that, in retrospect, it must have been his first ever game, even though he lost. Ryan doesn't understand. Of course, that's not what he meant.

"But just because I lost, doesn't mean I didn't pitch well. You can't control everything."

"That's true," Ryan says. "Yeah, I see." The song ends. Seventh inning stretch is done. Everyone sits down again.

In the top of the eighth the Tigers take the lead with two solo shots, and two back-to-back doubles. The Orioles push one more across in the ninth with a triple and single, but can't come up with anything more. They lose six to five. August lifts himself from his chair. His leg is asleep. Ryan reminds him about the note, and August says he'll just call them on the phone.

"Are you sure? We're right here."

"I'm sure. I'll call them. It's okay."

"Okay." They file out with everyone else. The mood isn't somber. It's just another game in a long season. It's just another day in a long series of days.

"Let's go get you some autographs," August says.

"Oh yeah, I almost forgot."

Outside the Orioles' gate fans gaggle in an anticipatory hush. The kids are mostly younger, with their fathers, a few mothers, some with older figures—brothers or friends—who can drive.

Some have balls, or bats, or posters, and some have baseball cards, and everybody has a pen. Ryan tells him that some people will try to sell the autographs, and the adults with plastic sheaths of pictures or cases of baseball cards could be those. Some kids with index cards, or scraps of paper could care less about that, August thinks. But most know about value. One kid in a red jacket comes up to August and Ryan and shows him his autographs, many of which are current Orioles players. August wonders why the kid needs any more. He must rely on the anonymity of his position as a fan.

The players materialize one at a time (in August's day they traveled in clumps—safety in numbers). Some sign a few items and drive off in their cars. Some players stand and sign an item for everybody, chat with the fans. A few of the players come out and say they have to be somewhere and don't sign a thing. Ryan gets about half of the players that come out. Most of the big stars that emerge don't sign a thing, except one. Ryan finds the right card and pulls it out, and runs over to where the player is, and gets it signed. August never used to sign autographs. He didn't see what the point of it was.

During the drive home the kid talks excitedly about the autographs. He has never gotten autographs before, he says. "This was great. Wow." August asks him how he became so enthralled with baseball if his father isn't interested in the sport really, and Ryan says he doesn't know. It just absorbed him for some reason. Most kids don't like the sport anymore, of course, he says. Everybody is into basketball or hockey and football. Eventually, August knows it will come back to baseball. Just give them time.

"What has happened with your father, with your father

and your mother?" The kid is still shuffling through his autographs. He doesn't look up.

"They're okay. This has happened lots of times, really."

"Really?"

"Yeah. They say they're not getting divorced. I don't know about that. I don't care really."

August doesn't buy this for a minute.

"Really?"

"No, not really." August says that his parents have both died, that his mother died when he was a kid. His father was lost to the world after that, he says.

"So you're saying I need—"

"I'm not really saying anything in particular. Just exist, that's all."

"Yeah," Ryan says. "How does it feel to drive again?"

"It feels fine. This car actually isn't that different from the one I used to have. I think it's a good car. I feel awkward, but it's okay."

"It doesn't feel like you're going to crash? You're not worried about hitting anyone?"

"No."

"That's good. Don't."

"You're right. Just don't," August says.

Zachary told them to call from the Interfaith Center when they were done. The sky is dark, and August is hungry. The lights in the parking lot have clicked on. The parking lot is full. Inside the Interfaith Center a reception is underway. People mill in the corridor, near the office, flap at the plants in the corridor, plastic drinks in hand. August and Ryan are both hungry. August parks in front of the building with the blinkers and they walk through the front entrance, into the office and call Zachary. There is no answer for five or six rings. When Zachary does pick it up his voice is muffled, and he's out of breath. August can hear a faint voice in the background. Sax, laughter.

"Zacky, I don't have that much time..." and then it trails off. A woman's voice.

"Hello?"

"Hello, Mr. Tulane?"

"Yes, August. How was everything?"

"Better than I thought actually. I think."

"Well that's good news. That's great," he says.

"Right, well I hope you enjoyed yourself. Is my renegade son there with you?"

"Yes, sir."

"And how did he—how was he for you?"

"Fine, fine." August can hear more muffling sounds, then change jingling, and the woman's voice again, although August can't make out what she says this time. Ryan is out in the corridor, watching some lady fix a button on her blouse.

"And the car's okay."

"We're here, waiting for you. The car's here. We're hungry, so—"

"I'll be right there," he says.

"Okay then."

August can see Ryan's immediate future and it is not pretty.

"Do you want to learn how to drive?" August and Ryan stand in the office, where the secretaries sit normally.

"Someday," Ryan says. "Next year I can get my driver's permit."

"Sure. That must be something you look forward to."

"Right, definitely. Freedom."

"You want to learn right now?"

"You mean on my mother's car?"

"Sure, why not?" Ryan looks out the office window, into the corridor, where yellow light and shadows move softly across the tiles. A smile swishes across his face. He seems surprised considering the possible ramifications. "We've got a few minutes."

"Okay," Ryan says. "Let's do it." They walk out of the office, lock it, step out through the corridor and outside. August hands him the keys, and Ryan sits in the driver's seat.

"This is a stick shift, so don't get scared," he says. "I'll walk you through it."

"Okay," Ryan says. He sits straight, back straight, hands tight against the wheel. He grips the stumpy sports car stick shift.

"What you need to do with a stick shift is press down on the clutch, and then turn the ignition. At the same time." Ryan looks at the clump of keys in his hand, says he's not sure which one it is. August picks the long one out, and hands it to Ryan. He slides it into the ignition. August can hear the metal of the key scrape against the metal of the inside of the ignition slot. Ryan looks at his feet. The radio plays some overproduced poppy rock number.

"Feel the clutch?" August tilts his head, peers down at the kid's feet.

"Yes," I do. "I think. It's the middle pedal, right?"

"No that's the brake. It's the pedal on the far, far left."

"Oh, okay."

"Okay?" Slowly Ryan pushes the pedal in with his foot.

"Okay, now hit the ignition." Ryan twists his hand quickly, and the engine fires. August reaches over and hits the emergency blinkers off. "We're in business."

"Yeah." A couple walks along the sidewalk towards the Interfaith Center and enters it. Another couple leaves.

"Good job, Ryan."

"Okay, okay. Now what?"

"Now's the intuition. It's all feel. It's in neutral now. Flip it into first. What you do is let the clutch up, and at the same time, give it a little bit of gas. Too much gas isn't good, and not enough isn't good."

"Cause it won't go."

"It'll stall. Make sure you give it enough to go. It takes practice." The car idles. Everything else is quiet. Ryan lifts the clutch; August can see his left leg rise, slowly.

"Hit the gas, hit the gas." Ryan does, but too late. The car jerks forward, and stalls. Ryan smiles. "It's okay, that's fine," August says. "Now you know what not to do. Now try it another way. Give it more, and quicker."

Ryan starts the car again, and lets it idle again in neutral.

"Can I lift my foot off it now?"

"Sure you can, yeah. It's in neutral. Just put in it first when you hold the clutch down."

"But can I hold the clutch down when it's in neutral?"

"Yeah, no problem." Ryan flips the gear into first while pressing the clutch in, and nods at August. "Okay."

"Okay. Give it a little more this time."

He lets the clutch out and at the same time gives it gas, much harder this time, and the car flies forward with a squeal. And Ryan's driving down the parking lot. August tells him to let up on the gas a little bit, claps him on the shoulder. They are moving in first gear, circling the parking lot. Ryan smiles ear to ear.

"You can shift into second now."

"I can?"

"Yeah, you can hear the engine. It's running too fast right now. It needs to be shifted." Ryan pushes down the clutch. August says that's what he should do. August takes Ryan's hand and puts it on the gearshift, and they shift into second together, on the far end of the parking lot in the dark.

8. Sunday

August lifts the bucket from beneath the storeroom sink and turns the hot water into the plastic bottom of the bucket. He squeezes soap into the cascade. He turns the hot water higher until the bubbles froth and rise to the lip of the bucket. He walks to the tack-board shelving behind the storeroom door and finds the rubber gloves—the thick orange gloves with the soft inner meshing. August places the bucket next to the shelving and wiggles the gloves on, trying not to touch the used outside of the glove with anything other than the plastic wrapping he tore when he opened the package. He works his fingers deep inside each glove until only a small pocket of air separates his finger from the tip and he stretches and pops the joints on his fingers inside as he reaches for a sponge and drops that in the bucket. Ripping leaf-print paper towels from the holster, he folds them into his back pocket.

He's down the hall to the women's room, and he knocks.

"Any ladies in here?" No answer. "Hello? Any ladies?"

No ladies. August pushes the door with his shoulder, careful not to jostle the water and soap in the bucket, and he's inside. He holds the door open with his foot, and takes the sign that reads "Cleaning in Process" from his pocket and props it in between the door and the door-stop. He locks the inner door. He will need to mop the floors today.

As he's walking down the corridor he can hear the Baptist choir singing "Just a Closer Walk with Thee." The far door is ajar, so that members might come in late. He has his spray bottle. He needs to tend to the plants today. August sprays the plants near the entrance of room four and peeks into the room. The chairs he set up are now filled with members of the church, and they are holding their hymnals out in front of them, and singing flat, off key, in vibrato, too slow, too fast. The sun and clouds are clear through the windows above them all. He has never interrupted a service for anything, and he won't do so today. This is sacred and what could be gained by going in, even out of curiosity?

As he's turning away, peeling from the door, a man dressed in the cloth bumps him accidentally coming in. Reverend Tannen is one of August's favorite people. He's a little man, bald with tallow skin, dark eyes the color of coffee. He carries a Bible, with tassels marking the important passages.

"Good morning August," he says. "I'm sorry."

"Oh, you did scare me. Good morning. Are you running

late this morning?"

"Yes, I am. But you know, they go on without me just fine I think." The reverend has stopped and seems willing to speak with August until the hymn is over, and he can enter with the appropriate authority.

"Right, they usually go on without me too."

"Which is part of life, I think. Just realizing that we're really all replaceable. That's why each day is so important." August believes this to be true, a philosophy worth living. The reverend shakes August's hand as the hymn is winding down, and August says he is glad the Interfaith Center has people like him around, and that people are his favorite part of the job.

"August, you do a wonderful job around here," the reverend says. "I hope you are good to yourself today."

"I will try my best, reverend," he says. "Thank you."

"That's all anyone wants," he says. "An effort."

When he enters the door, August watches the heads turn in appreciation. The reverend blinks at August and heads down the aisle towards the podium.

At the end of the day August walks home. Sundays are really his favorite days—the sense of lethargy and muted expectations. Low expectations. He knows he won't have many obligations aside from the absolute necessities. He takes the long way home today, through the Village center, and by the lake. The sun burns low in the sky, and it feels cooler than it has been.

The marshy area surrounding the lake is abuzz with birds clicking in the weeds. He finds a clump of pussy willow and picks one. He will put it in a glass, on his table. Focusing on the little things in life helps make the bigger ones stay big, adds a texture that he thinks he needs to do better with. Why does he worry so much about what has been and what will be? These things aren't really important enough to warrant the attention. What is, is exactly this—today and the moments of it strung together.

When he gets home he calls the Orioles' office. He tells the secretary who he is and she forwards his call to a manager in the front office. The man sounds genuinely willing to help, and eager to meet August face to face. Now he is part of a history, not just in his mind. But the more he talks to the man, the less it feels like the right thing. He has a life, and it's a good life, or at least it is what it is—what he wants it to be. Towards the end of the conversation the man says that surely the Orioles could come up with something for him, but that is also the moment when he realizes that he has much more to do before he could make that kind of change. Maybe when he has retired, he thinks. Something more along the lines of a more permanent change.

"What do you think, Mr. Griffin?"

"You have been very kind. Thank you again for that. I actually, I didn't plan on this. I changed my mind about what I want, I think. I'll think over what you said, but I also think I need to be here for a while longer, although like I said I'll give your words some thought."

"I'd still love to meet you, August."

"I'd like to meet you too, son."

After dinner he stands at the sink and does his dishes. He watches the soap bubble in the sink of dishes, and listens to the local news. A man was shot dead in Washington, and another man is missing in Virginia. An eight-car pileup developed late last night when an eighteen-wheeler slammed into a van on the highway, and the other cars plowed into them. There is a stray cat problem in Baltimore and hundreds of cats have to be put to sleep. August closes his eyes for a moment. The loss of life.

August knows he is a man like many other men, and yet unlike them partially. He has something to offer the world, and it's the ordinary days that bring that out, whatever it is. How much he would listen to Vick's advice, he doesn't know. Maybe it would be better to change locales and live in a different building for a while, one that is further away, buy a car, assemble himself into a more manageable package. But then again, maybe only muted adjustments are needed. An altered mind-set, not an altered frame of reference. August isn't wielding answers.

For tonight this is enough: watching television on the sofa, head resting against a pillow, feet propped on the arm of the sofa, a glass of water, some butter cookies, losing consciousness in the flickering lights. The volume turned down low to a murmur.

About the Author

Nathan Leslie's nine previous books of fiction include *Root and Shoot, Sibs* and *Drivers*. Nathan published *Root and Shoot* in 2015 with Texture Press. He is also the author of *The Tall Tale of Tommy Twice*, a novel, and the poetry collection *Night Sweat* and his work has appeared in hundreds of literary magazines including *Boulevard, Shenandoah, North American Review,* and *Cimarron Review*. Nathan was series editor for *The Best of the Web* anthology 2008 and 2009 (Dzanc Books) and edited fiction for *Pedestal Magazine* for many years. He is currently interviews editor at *Prick of the Spindle* and he writes a monthly music column for *Atticus Review*. His work appeared in *Best Small Fictions 2016*. Check him out on Twitter and Facebook as well as at www.nathanleslie.com.